Tears of a FATHER

Tears of a Father

tellwell

Tellwell Talent

www.tellwell.ca

ISBN

978-0-2288-0808-4 (Paperback)

TABLE OF CONTENTS

CHAPTER ONE

The golden streak on the eastern horizon heralded the dawn of another day. A cool, misty breeze brought the light smell of decaying sugar cane and scorched soil. This breeze refreshed any morning walker who braved the cool air and the darkness that still engulfed the sugar cane village. The chirping of the birds and the crowing of the roosters further announced the birth of a new day.

A sudden howling of dogs beside the compound jolted fifty-year-old Mahesh from his bed. With eyes half open, he tried to gaze through the frosty glass pane of his bedroom window. A herd of his neighbour's cattle was passing through and making his dogs go wild. Mahesh, a medium-built person with greying hair was the pillar of his small family. His wife perished in a hurricane that ripped through the Fijian islands. His eldest son settled in the United States after marriage. Mahesh lived with his only daughter in the small family house on the farm.

He opened the window. A cool breeze blew over his face and rattled the photos and calendar that decorated the back wall. His eyes caught the smiling face of his wife staring back at him from one of the frames. A tinge of sadness crossed his face.

It was as if she was trying to tell him something. Her shining, beautiful eyes set in a round face gave her the look of a young girl. A tendril of black hair curled over her forehead, which had given her the nickname of Curly.

Mahesh's gaze suddenly became hazy, as he drifted down the memory lane . . .

***

A cloud of dust loomed over the dirt track that linked his house to the main road. The Benai Road meandered between the sugar cane fields and was the only link to the Ba main town. A sound like that of horses on the loose echoed across the dense sugar cane plantation. It was, in fact, a pack of goats that was creating such chaos. A cry of help amidst the disturbance pierced through the bushy vegetation. It was unmistakably the cry of a girl in distress.

"Help! Help!"

Mahesh, then a young man in his early twenties, rushed toward the source of the sound. Barefoot, he ran on the uneven silty track between the cane lands. He fell several times but got back on foot and kept running as if he was being chased by a cougar. The next bend afforded him a blurry view of several goats bleating and running. The girl's agonized cry made him run faster. He was almost out of breath when he reached the last of the animals.

The scene was ghastly.

A young woman of around nineteen was trying to pull the animal to a stop. She was fervently trying to pull the rope that the animal was tethered in.

Mahesh shouted, "Just leave the rope. Leave the rope!"

His shouts fell on deaf ears. He was almost at the side of the running girl and he again shouted, "Leave the rope! Are you mad?"

It was then he realized that the rope had somehow gotten entangled around her hand and the girl could not free herself from the noose.

Her wrist was bleeding profusely. Mahesh took hold of the rope and applied all his strength to his feet. The animal appeared to be big and strong. He was no match for that goat. He was concerned about the safety of the girl, who was about to fall.

With one hand he grasped the rope whilst with the other he swiftly took out a small penknife from his pocket and cut the rope loose, freeing the girl from the panicked animal. He also let go off the rope and gently lay the girl on his lap.

She was almost unconscious. Her beautiful face and long, plaited black hair mesmerized him. She was wet with the perspiration that soaked her completely.

Mahesh was still wondering who this pretty lass was when several voices, followed by running footsteps, distracted him.

A crying middle-aged woman was coming toward him.

"Oh, my child. Oh, my child. What happened to my Curly?"

She quickly took her from my arms and started kissing her. By this time, several nearby labourers had come to her aid. For several minutes she lay motionless. At last, she opened her eyes, much to the relief of the villagers. All eyes were on the girl lying in her mum's arms. No one seemed to notice Mahesh or the injuries he sustained whilst helping her.

Gradually, the crowd faded, leaving him seated on an outcrop of rock under a mango tree. He was also sweating, despite the cool morning air. He couldn't erase the girl's face from his mind. *Who is she?* He wondered.

Some two weeks later, when Mahesh was returning from his farm, he was suddenly confronted by the same girl.

He saw the same beautiful face with a lock of black hair curling on her forehead. His heart started pounding heavily and suddenly he found his mouth drying up. What was happening to him?

The girl came face-to-face with him and politely said, "I just don't know how to thank you. You saved my life by risking yours. You must be a messiah."

Mahesh shook his head. "No, no, it is okay. Every person has a moral obligation. I just did what any other person would have done."

She blushed slightly and added, "My name is Karishma. Friends and loved ones call me 'Curly.' I have not seen you before. Which family do you come from? You must have a name?" she said, smiling.

Mahesh blushed. He did not know how to talk to a beautiful girl.

"Oh yeah, sure. I am Mahesh Prasad. I lost my parents a long time back and am looking after the small sugar cane farm my father left. I live with my distant relatives." He pointed to a clutter of houses amidst the trees.

"Oh, so you are from the family who lives near the creek. My dad is Pundit Shambhu Kashyap. He is the head pundit of the Benai Temple."

Mahesh did not know why this information came as a blow to him. He only knew that the family of the pundit did not get along well with his relatives due to an ongoing land dispute. The thought irked him. But why?

Karishma put her hand on his hand and said, "You are the best person I have ever met in my life." She looked so beautiful. Her innocent face was full of passion and gratitude.

She held his hand and looked straight in his eyes. Her eyes captivated him. They reminded him of the deep blue sea near the Yasawas.

They stood there with their eyes locked, unaware of the scorching heat, as if talking through their eyes. A familiar voice all of a sudden woke him up from his fantasy.

***

"Papa. Papa. Papa."

He felt someone shaking him violently. It was his daughter, Meenakshi. "Papa, your breakfast is ready."

He became embarrassed when he saw his smiling daughter looking at him. She was a replica of her late mum, both in looks and personality.

Mahesh hurriedly made his way to the bathroom. After refreshing himself, he joined his daughter at the dining table.

"Papa, Raju called me late at night. He and Bhabhi"—his sister-in-law—"have seen a suitable boy for me. He has sent the picture of the boy to my cell phone."

Mahesh looked at the photo of a tall, slim boy with a smiling face. "He works with Raju as a salesman. Only his disabled mum lives with him. Papa, I like him. He has phoned me several times and is ready to marry me. In fact, he is already in Fiji."

"Oh?" Mahesh inquired.

"Papa, he will be coming to meet us this Saturday,"

Mahesh inwardly cursed himself for not finding a match for his daughter here in Fiji. It was his and his wife's intention to have their daughter settle in Fiji. But now destiny was dictating otherwise.

Their eldest son migrated to Czekeland several years back. After moving away, his attitude changed and he was now like a stranger to Mahesh. Mahesh did not want to lose his daughter. She was the youngest and was very close to him. But he could not let this opportunity slip away from his daughter. Her happiness meant everything to him.

Saturday afternoon saw both families sit down in a cordial atmosphere. The boy, whose name was Som, appeared to be very gentle and nice. Both parties agreed to the relationship, and it was a year later, when Meena received her visa for Czekeland, that the actual marriage took place.

The departure of her daughter left him lonely. She was the only one with whom he shared his pain and grief. He was, however, satisfied that Meena was happy with her married life.

She often called him. Two years passed, and only upon Meena's continuous insistence did he agree to accept and complete the migration papers. He did not want to leave the island as he had lots of memories here.

Mahesh sat on the patio, sipping a bowl of *kava*, a traditional Fijian drink.

Unwittingly, he again began to travel down the memory lane. His thoughts rested on the goat incident, where he had saved Curly from the scared animal.

***

He remembered how deeply Curly loved him. Her parents were totally against this relationship. They even refused his marriage proposal. Having no other choice, he and Curly went to Lautoka, a city approximately forty kilometres west of his residence, and they had a courthouse marriage, which they followed with Hindu marriage rituals in the temple. Mahesh really admired his wife's guts, as she was not only brave but positive in every aspect of life.

Although Mahesh was not a rich man, he still earned enough from his farm to make ends meet. He remembered the difficult time when his eldest son, Raju, was in college. In addition to expenses for a school uniform, socks and shoes, he also had to fork out money for bus fare.

Every year, he had to make an upfront deposit to the school, on top of which were building fees and other related school expenses. At times, he had to borrow money from some of his friends to pay for Raju's needs.

Mahesh wanted to see his children educated and on their feet. He went through some really tough times. His only concern was their education. He used to work for his neighbours' farms after his own work was done to earn a few extra dollars.

It was customary for the family to have vegetarian meals every Tuesday and Friday.

They had a family temple built adjacent to the house and every morning Raju used to pray before going to school. Every Saturday, he would offer water to Lord Sun and Lord Hanuman. He was an ardent devotee of Lord Hanuman (a Hindu god).

The family's culture and in-house traditions were very well respected and adhered to by the kids. Raju was regarded as one the best students at his college. The village folks also liked him and often praised him for being so decent and cultured.

Meena was equally religious and cultured—a typical Indian girl. She was highly disciplined and strictly observed all the rituals and practices of the family. After the demise of her mum, she had no choice but to opt out of schooling.

Mahesh was still was hurt by the words of his father-in-law, the village pundit (priest). He could vividly recall what the pundit said when he approached him for his blessing of their marriage. "Look at your status. You are a low-caste person. Don't even dream of coming near to my daughter."

These words stung him like a bee. He pleaded with him. "Please, Pundit. I have never engaged in bad deeds. I always pray to the Almighty and do my best to help the others. You can ask the village folks. Is it my fault that I was born in a low-caste family? You are educated and know about our scriptures. Gita and Ramayana (Hindu scriptures) have clearly stipulated that there is no caste. A person is big or small because of his deeds."

The pundit retorted, "You are trying to teach me? Get the heck out of here now, before I throw you out."

Mahesh became furious, and before anger could entirely engulf him, he walked out, humiliated.

It was not that he was scared; he did it for the good of his Curly. Mahesh had a lot of respect in the community.

Both young and old liked him. For some, he was their mentor. To be castrated and ridiculed in this manner was just unacceptable.

The next day, early in the morning, Curly called. She sobbed into the phone, "I did not know that my dad was such a ruthless person. Please, dear, accept my apologies for my dad's behaviour. Please, please."

Mahesh held the phone, becoming equally emotional. It took almost one hour for him to console her, but when he told Curly to forget him, she was adamant that she wouldn't and said, "You are my first and last love. My dad wants me to marry a foreigner and I overheard him telling Mum that the marriage will take place within a month. By then, if you do not make me your own, you will never see me alive again." She hung up the phone.

Mahesh stood speechless, his mouth dry. Instinct warned him that something terrible was about to happen. He knew that Curly never lied. So, he was left with two options: elope with Curly or let her commit suicide. Mahesh was a very disciplined and cultured Indian man. In his culture, it was forbidden to have unethical relationships with another.

What will the society say? He brooded. The respect that he had now would be gone in no time if he did something that society did not embrace. Without eloping, there was no other way, because Mahesh did not want to go against the principles he adhered to and preached. If he did not bring Curly with him, she would kill herself. The thought brought a chill to his spines.

She didn't call him for the next two days. He tried to call her, but whenever he called, there was no answer. Two days elapsed and Mahesh started getting worried.

Late that night he heard the dogs barking. Dogs' barking was common in the villages, but when the barking went on for a long time, it meant that someone was outside his house.

There was a sound of hurried footsteps followed by desperate knocking on his door. He quickly took a torch and a penknife he carried at night in case of animal attacks and rushed to see who it was.

With his heart pounding heavily, he glanced through the window curtains but could not see who was there. He waited, and all of a sudden the dogs stopped barking and the knocking stopped. The silence was eerie.

Then the banging started up again, but this time it was much louder. It was a non-stop barrage. Without thinking, Mahesh flung the door open. The sight that met his eyes sent a cold shiver down his body. It was Curly.

She was clad in a bloodstained dress. Her hair was shabby and her eyes looked startled. Without saying anything, she rushed into Mahesh's arms and started sobbing like a child. Mahesh quickly closed the door and placed his hand on her head. He caressed her, and, while saying comforting words made her sit on the couch. Blood was oozing from her hands. Upon inquiry, it was revealed that Curly had cut her arms with a sharp razor. With that blade, she actually tried to carve the initials "MP," meaning Mahesh Prasad. Her mother slapped her twice for what she did. She was also rebuked by her dad and warned to stay clear of Mahesh. Mahesh boiled some water and nursed her cuts, dipping spirits on the inflicted area. He bandaged it properly.

"Let's go," Mahesh said angrily.

"Where?" Curly looked surprised.

"Your house. I will drop you back at your house now before anyone sees you."

"No. I have come here to stay for good. It is another thing if you do not want me."

"No. No. No," Mahesh retorted. "Please try to understand me, my dear. We cannot stay together without getting married. It is against our society's rules, and our religious beliefs do not allow it."

"What society rules are you talking about? The society where girls do not have a right to choose their husbands? The society which discriminates on the grounds of caste and status? Mahesh, I have told you that if I ever marry, it will be to you, otherwise I will remain single for my lifetime."

Mahesh wanted to say something but Curly continued, "If my dad forces me to marry someone else, there will be a disaster no one anticipated."

Mahesh was spellbound; he knew perfectly well that he needed to make a fast decision. It was evident now that Curly was getting desperate. Mahesh again tried to reason out with her. "Curly, please. I also love you and want to marry you. But let us do this in a proper manner. To develop a relationship like this is just unethical. Let me drop you at home now, and I promise that tomorrow we will find a way."

She recoiled. “Tomorrow? There is no tomorrow, Mahesh. Promise me that tomorrow you will take me to Lautoka (a small city) to have our marriage endorsed. If you give me your word, I will go back now. Otherwise, I will go back and never return. It is a promise.”

Mahesh was stunned for a moment. He felt his legs giving way. His hands trembled. He wondered whether this was the right thing to do. Marrying Curly in secrecy meant he would be going against the rules of his society. He would lose all the respect and recognition he had gained through his virtues. People would mock and ridicule him. On the other hand, he thought he could not let a young girl who loved him more than this world take her life because of his rejection. After weighing the pros and cons he finally agreed.

“Okay, Curly. Tomorrow morning you need to take your belongings and be ready. As soon as I call, just come outside, near the road. I will pick you from there.”

Their secret marriage infuriated Curly’s family but they could not do much. One or two villagers who were against this marriage later befriended Mahesh when they came to know the circumstances which forced them to marry this way.

***

Mahesh lay on the couch for several hours, thinking about his past, unaware that night had fallen. The buzzing of the mosquitoes woke him up. He looked up at the clear sky and the silver moon, which was high in the sky, giving off the only light. He heaved a sigh of relief and wished that Curly had been alive. The next couple of days saw him quite busy, since his visa had arrived and he needed to make the preparations for his flight. The thought of leaving this place saddened him. He was too attached to the lifetime of memories this farm and this place held. But he wanted to see his daughter, his son and the grandkids.

If one stays in a particular place for over fifty years, the place, the earth, the air and the surroundings become a part of him. Even the smell of the place carried a flood of memories. Mahesh bid goodbye to his friends and relatives. He asked his second cousin to look after his farm and house. Although he had no blood relatives left in the village, he still felt very emotional. The fond childhood memories, the time he spent with Curly, the events and festivals he attended in the village and the dancing and merrymaking all came flooding back to him. The fond memories of villagers, his farm and his house all contributed to the rolling tears he could not control. He was overwhelmed with emotion and wished he could stay there forever.

Once in the aircraft, he felt much better. He felt guilty; however, as Curly always told him not to ever leave that country. This thought saddened him.

The way Raju changed after going abroad really hurt her. She did not want him and Meena to follow Raju's footsteps. She wanted their children to adhere to the cultures and traditions their forefathers preached. Before her death, she repeatedly told Mahesh that once in a foreign land, people tend to lose their grip on their social and religious beliefs. Apart from Raju there were many other people in the family who had done likewise. This was one of the reasons she did not want them to migrate to Western countries. But Mahesh had no options left. Meena chose her husband, and he, as her father, respected her decision. He was not one of those who forced their children to marry someone of their parents' choice only. He had liberal views and believed that parents should only guide their youngsters. No parent should ever impose things on their children— especially not those who were mature enough to stand on their own feet.

The view from the plane was so beautiful. It looked like a Diwali festival (Festival of Lights) on the ground. The glimmer of the lights and the awe-inspiring view thrilled Mahesh.

The pilot's voice came on over the intercom. "Ladies and gentlemen, this is your captain. Welcome to Czekeland Airport. As we start our descent, please make sure your seat belts are buckled and tray tables are in their full upright position. Also, please turn off all electronic devices until we are safely on the ground. Thank you all for flying with us. Enjoy your stay."

Mahesh had always heard of the vastness of these cities. The sight that met his eyes from the airplane was much more than he could have imagined. It was not only vast, but highly organized, as well. He could see tiny roads crisscrossing the ground from one end to the other. The various colours of lights on the ground in an array of pathways were very captivating. For a moment, Mahesh became lost in the spectacular scenery.

His heart pounded heavily as he made his way past the final gate. The thought of seeing his daughter made him walk faster and faster. There were hundreds of people in the arrivals reception area. Mahesh got a bit nervous and started scrutinizing the faces of all the people who were gathered there. He could not see his daughter. *Where is she?* He wondered.

She was to pick him up from the airport. He waited for some time but there was no sign of her. He felt his heart sinking. What if she didn't come? He didn't even know where she lived. All of a sudden, his thoughts were interrupted by a familiar voice. "Papa! Papa!"

As he turned around, his daughter ran into his arms. He left his luggage and hugged Meena. Tears rolled down the cheeks of both daughter and father.

His happy tears soaked his shirt. After he got a hold of himself, he looked at Meena. She was more beautiful than before. Her black hair flowed over her shoulders and her enticing dark blue eyes gazed at him with affection. She was a carbon copy of her mum.

"How was the trip, Dad? Did you like the plane ride? Were you afraid? Did you eat anything?"

Meena's barrage of questions made Mahesh laugh. She was bubbling over with excitement. In that excitement she seemed to have forgotten that her husband, Som, was also there.

Som welcomed Mahesh warmly and picked up his luggage. They were about to exit the terminal when a big-bellied man with shabby hair and ripped jeans appeared in front of them. It was none other than Raju.

He smiled and shook hands with Mahesh. Giving the man a puzzled look, Mahesh stopped in his tracks. He looked at the man closely and eventually recognized his son.

They hugged each other and Mahesh was once again on the verge of tears since the last time he saw Raju, Curly was still alive. *What has happened to Raju?* He wondered. He was such a handsome boy, slim and always smiling. Today he looked older than Mahesh. The clothes he wore were smelly and dirty. Maybe this was the way people dressed here, Mahesh mused inwardly. Raju's normally calm and pleasant demeanor was missing. Worry lines marred his forehead. His face was pale and smeared with dirt. Fine streaks of grey flecked his hair on the temples.

Raju looked back and signaled someone. It was a young woman whose features resembled Meena's. With a smiling face, she came toward him.

"Hello, Grandpa," she said.

Mahesh was initially confused, but now he remembered the girl as Raju's daughter. He saw her in the only photo Raju had sent to them since he had left the island.

Mahesh took the girl in his arms. This was the first time he had met his granddaughter. She was now a college student with another year before she graduated and became a doctor. Even though she had been born and bred in Czekeland, she appeared very humble and cultured. Even her attire reflected this. Mahek was her name. Mahesh felt so relieved to see his granddaughter. He had lost all hope of seeing Raju and his family ever again.

It was a fairly warm day in Czekeland. The busy city was bustling with heavy, bumper-to-bumper traffic, which amused Mahesh. He wondered how people drove in that congestion. After several hours of driving, the car pulled up to a big house with a vast compound. The rays of the setting sun reflected off the windowpanes.

It was a beautiful house. Mahesh was a given a separate suite with all the facilities he had ever dreamed of. Raju and Mahek also joined them. That night over dinner, they talked and talked amidst laughter and merrymaking. It was a great family reunion.

All of a sudden, Mahesh turned toward Raju and said. "Where is Sally, Raju?" Sally was Raju's wife.

Raju and Mahek looked at each other. He hesitated.

"She is at work, Dad. She will come and meet you once she is free," he said with a sullen face. There was a tinge of sadness in his voice.

Their conversation after that ranged from the lifestyle in Fiji to the current status of Fijian immigrants overseas. Mahek was very vocal and her opinions on the lifestyle there indicated to Mahesh that they now felt they were in heaven. But he was not convinced. He still thought that it was the other way around. Meena, although happy, was quiet on these issues. Before returning home, Raju and Mahek approached Mahesh.

"Dad, I think it would be best if you came to our place and stayed there. We have a separate bedroom with all the facilities. You will be happy with us."

Mahesh's gaze rested on Raju. He studied his son's serious face, surprised to hear that he wanted him to stay

at his house. He wondered how a son who had
any love toward his parents for more than a de
seemed to care.

Mahek interjected, "Yes, Grandpa, we would love to have you there. After school tomorrow, I will take you for a walk and then you can tell me all the ghost stories of Fiji."

Mahesh was silent. This was the first time he had met his granddaughter and she talked as if she had known him forever. Well, she was his own blood, he thought. Raju must have told her lots of tales of Fiji.

Raju looked inquiringly at his dad. "Well, what do you think, Dad?"

After giving it some more thought, he replied, "Let's talk about it later on, Raju. I will stay here for the night. See you tomorrow."

Inwardly, Mahesh was very happy about his son's invitation since he believed that it was unethical for parents to eat and sleep in the house of their daughter and son-in-law. Indian customs had certain policies which, if not adhered to, meant a rebuke from society. Mahesh remembered how one of his villagers, Damodar, was ousted from their community just because he chose to stay with his son-in-law. He was rebuffed and became a victim of sarcastic comments by his neighbors.

Mahesh shut his eyes, enjoying the softness of the bed, the smoothness of his blanket. He was so tired that as soon as his head touched the pillow, sleep overcame him. He must have slept for some eight hours. The sun was up. He was surprised that not even the usual chirping of birds nor the sound of traffic on the nearby highway had disturbed his deep slumber. Then again, this could be attributed to the time difference between Fiji and the Czekeland.

It was the sound of the bell and the chanting of mantras that finally woke him. He thought he was dreaming, but when the fragrance from the incense sticks began to nauseate him, he knew that someone was praying. The structures of the houses in the northern hemisphere were quite different from those in tropical countries. All houses had to stand up to the severe cold season that befell these places. Meena and Som's was a closed-type house with hardly any windows that opened because of the chilliness that still shrouded the Czekeland valley. This was why the aroma from the incense sticks filled the house inside.

Although Czekeland did not experience the severe winter that other cities did, the houses still had to be built in a way to thwart the cold in the winter and the heat in the summer. This house was apparently no exception. While lying in bed, Mahesh thought of the uniqueness of this place: no dogs barking, no high-volume radios buzzing. An atmosphere totally different from that in Fiji.

Mahesh's thoughts reverted to what Raju said last night. He wondered whether he really meant it. Mahek was a darling, and the urge to get to know her helped him to decide the best option for him.

He switched on the TV and was enjoying a religious serial when a faint squeaking sound disturbed him. It sounded like two metal objects scraping against each other. The sound gradually became louder and stopped outside his bedroom door. Mahesh wondered what it could be. Before he could get out of the bed, the door was flung open with a heavy bang.

What he saw in the doorway almost took his breath away. It was a fragile-looking, hideous, old woman sitting in a wheelchair. She had a large *nose shaped* like the beak of a *raven and l*ong, untidy silver-brown hair that flowed over her shoulders. Hooded red anguished eyes popped out of a face that was lacerated with wrinkles. Her bushy grey eyebrows almost covered her eyes, giving her the look of a hag. She was very scary indeed. With thin and bloodless lips showing two teeth protruding from her ugly mouth, her angry eyes rested on Mahesh. Mahesh could not meet her stare and shifted his gaze.

For a moment, she just glared at him and there was a chilling silence. Even the wind seemed to have stopped howling. Mahesh felt very uneasy. Only the ticking of a clock and a bird calling far in the distance could be heard in that tense atmosphere. The silence was finally broken by a raspy, wheezing voice.

"Who are you?" she hissed. Her voice was barely audible.

She flicked her tongue along her lips as if enjoying the moment. Mahesh was thrown aback. His voice seemed to have stuck in his throat. He felt his mouth go dry as he stared back at this old lady. She rasped again, "I am talking to you. Who are you and what are you doing in my house?" Mahesh was puzzled but gradually realized that this must be Som's disabled mum whom Meena had told him about earlier.

Mahesh was about to respond when a familiar voice cut in. It was Meena. "Mum, this is my dad. He arrived from Fiji last night."

The old, frail lady appeared not to have heard her. She looked tired and exhausted. Her hands were trembling. Without turning her head, she recoiled. "So what? Every person in this house has to be awake before five in the morning. When I start my praying, I don't want anyone lying in bed, nor do I want any TVs or radios switched on."

Mahesh was shocked to hear her speak so rudely. She kept staring at him, much to his discomfort.

"In this house, rules are rules. You better tell your dad our house rules. If he can't follow them, he can leave," she retorted.

Mahesh did not expect this type of behaviour from Som's mother. It was highly offensive and hardly ever seen in his community. Mahesh came from a society which always gave priority to any visitors at home. They believed that all guests should be given the same respect that one would give the Almighty. Even their enemies were regarded with respect and affection if they ever came to their houses.

The unpleasant behaviour on the part of his host upset Mahesh. But he did not show the frustration or anger he felt. Meena quickly made her way to the old lady and was about to grab the handle of the wheelchair when, once again, the old lady lashed out.

"No! I have told you many times not to come near me and my wheelchair, Meena. I do not want you to touch any of my belongings. How many times do I have to tell you that I am a *brahmini* (upper-caste female)."

Meena looked dumbfounded. She just stood there with tears in her eyes. But she was also trained to have complete self-control in all situations, just like her dad. Mahesh was very confident in this ability. From childhood, their kids were taught the importance of traditional and cultural values. The society in which Mahesh lived demanded that elders not be talked back to under any circumstances. They were to be respected and listened to at all times. These virtues made Meena remain silent and calm. Without further ado, the old hag quickly retreated. There was a moment of silence before Meena spoke.

"Dad, my mother-in-law has been like this from the very beginning. She thinks that people born in the upper caste are always above others."

"My dear, she is wrong." Mahesh said. "She still holds the archaic views many old people hold in regard to our faith and culture. No one is above anyone else. It is their deeds that make a person big or small."

"Yes, Dad, you have told us that many times. I remember everything you and Mum have taught me. We call her 'Granny.' She gets very happy when we call her that."

Mahesh smiled and looked at his daughter with fatherly affection. He just hoped that Raju also practised those moral values.

During their late breakfast, Granny could not be seen. According to Meena, she always skipped breakfast and retreated to her own room. Mahesh was still worried and inquired, “Meena, how do you manage to deal with your granny? Is this the way she treats everyone here?”

Meena smiled and her gazed shifted to her mother-in-law’s bedroom. “Dad, there is much more to it than meets the eye.” She lowered her voice and continued. “Had there been anyone else in my place, she would have gone away a long time back. Even Som is fed up with his own mum. She still adheres to the old ways and practices. We are all required to wake up before five in the morning and have our bath. No one is allowed to be in bed when she starts praying.”

Meena looked annoyed but continued. “At times we work late shifts and don’t go to sleep until after midnight, yet we are still required to wake up before five in the morning. She still believes in upper and lower castes—that is why she does not even take a glass of water from me. She says that I belong to a lower caste.”

Meena was on the verge of crying when Mahesh interjected. “It is okay, Meena. Most of the old fogeys still believe in old practices that are possible back in Fiji, but not here. I am so happy that you have been able to endure the hardships without complaining.”

Raju came later in the day and took his dad to go sightseeing. In the evening, he dropped him off at a temple where Fijians normally went. Mahesh saw many people whom he knew and was pleased to learn that people from

Fiji also did lots of worshipping and maintained their culture and religion in this Western country.

Mahesh stayed with his daughter and Som for almost two months. In this period, he came to know a lot about the lifestyle in Czekeland. He even made some friends. Raju would come almost every week and take him to places that Mahesh wanted to visit.

One evening while having dinner, Mahesh asked his daughter, "Meena, Granny never comes to eat with us and I have never seen you serving her food."

Som interrupted him. "Dad, she will not eat anything Meena gives her. She has hired her own maid who comes here every day to cook and serve her only."

All this time, Mahesh had wondered who that lady was. He saw her almost every day and thought that she came to help Meena with household chores. In fact, all this time he had been happy to think that Meena was well looked after, as she was pregnant.

Meena looked up inquiringly at Som with her eyes flashing. It was evident that she did not want her dad to know more about Granny's behaviour. Som continued, "Dad, I am really sorry that Mum insulted you the first day you arrived. I never really had a chance to apologize earlier."

Mahesh cut him short. "It's okay, son. I understand. She is old and has her own ideals. I was not offended at all." He said this although, inwardly, he had been hurt.

***

One day when Som was away at work, Mahesh told Meena that he wanted to stay with Raju. Meena was very much surprised and angry. Her eyes blazed at Mahesh.

"Dad, don't even think of that. If you want to visit him, I will take you there, but stay with them, no. No. No. No."

"But why?" Mahesh responded.

"Because of Raju's wife, Sally," she said. "Dad, I'm sorry to have to say it, but why do you think she didn't come to meet you? She is not a woman, Dad. She is more of a vulture."

Mahesh looked at Meena, who was trying to control her anger. Her flaming eyes spoke volumes. This was the first time he had seen Meena in a fit of rage. Mahesh wondered what had gone wrong between them. Were they not on speaking terms? And if not, then why?

Out of the corner of his eye, he saw Meena looking pale and dejected. "Dad, I know you don't feel comfortable here due to Mum's attitude. But that is just her nature."

Mahesh became silent for a while and then explained to Meena the reason he wanted to stay with Raju.

"You know, Meena, no matter what, Raju is my son. He also wants to spend time with his dad. Maybe he regrets what he did in the past. Mahek is also there, craving some time with me. I assure you that if they do not look after me well, I will be back."

Meena walked away from him and later, when Raju came, it was decided that Mahesh would stay with him.

***

Raju's was a big house—the kind in which most American kids dream of growing up. Secluded among trees and overlooking an undulating landscape, it had several balconies, a screened-in front porch, three detached garages, and, above all, a private swimming pool. It looked more like a palace than a house. A big driveway surrounded by tall shrubs led to the front of the house. Mahesh alighted from the car. There was a fairly big lawn but it appeared to have been neglected as weeds now covered sections of it. A wire fence bordered the property, sagging at spots where the wind had knocked it down.

Raju took Mahesh across a wide hallway, adjacent to which was a spacious living room. It had a seventy-eight-inch TV and a computer set at the far end. There was a small refrigerator and a microwave in the other corner. Three big sofas rested in the middle of the living room.

The walls were decorated with an array of photo in frames. He stood for a moment and saw pictures of Sally's mum and dad, and her brothers and sisters. He felt a bit sad that they did not have the courtesy to hang Curly's photo up there. But that should not matter, he consoled himself. A spiral staircase led upstairs, where he found three adjacent bedrooms. There were two more rooms visible at the far end of the floor.

Raju took his luggage to one of the rooms. It was sparsely furnished and the windows overlooked the scenic view. The rolling hills further enhanced the beauty of the landscape, giving it the appearance of a countryside retreat.

"Dad, why don't you get changed and freshen up? I will be back in an hour."

Mahesh started to like the place. One morning, he was looking outside his bedroom window when the sudden toot of a car made him jump. He hastily opened the bedroom door and crashed into someone. The collision floored both of them.

"You idiot. Are you blind?" a harsh voice snapped.

Mahesh got up apologetically, and, to his surprise, saw that it was none other than Sally. He went to help lift her up, but she rebuked him. "Leave me alone, you jerk. I don't know why Raju has to bring any Tom, Dick or Harry into my house."

Mahesh was stunned. Sally had a completely different look to her. She was attired in gothic clothing and wore a black hat that covered most of her head. Her beautiful long black hair had been replaced by short, mercury-red-coloured hair. She didn't possess the same demure personality he was accustomed to. It had been replaced by an arrogant and pompous attitude—the kind of personality that rich, egotistical women possessed.

She hurriedly got up and left the house, slamming the front door behind her.

Raju had gone out earlier, saying that Sally would take care of him and that she would also prepare lunch. Mahesh felt hungry and looked in the kitchen and the fridge. The only thing he found was some ice cream and some apples. He was about to eat when Mahek came back from the library. She flung herself into his arms.

"When did you get here, Grandpa? Dad didn't tell me you were coming or I would have stayed home. So nice to see you here, Grandpa." She turned and called to her mum. "Mummy! Mummy!"

"Your mum has gone out, Mahek. I do not know where, but I believe someone came to pick her up."

"Oh my god . . . Grandpa. Didn't she know that you're here?" She looked in the kitchen and found only dirty utensils lying in the sink. There was no food at all. Mahek quickly prepared some rice and lentils laced with spicy coriander. She also prepared some potatoes with onions. Mahesh was astonished to see the speed at which Mahek, the schoolgirl, prepared these dishes. He felt proud of her. They later had late lunch together, and, after asking Mahesh to rest, she went back to the library for her research work.

Her ambition to become a doctor would materialize very soon as this was her final year before graduation. Mahesh decided to take a nap. He was dozing off in his bedroom when the chime of the doorbell rang. He opened the door to see a beautiful middle-aged woman standing in the doorway.

"May I help you?" he asked. A smile flashed on the face of the woman. She was indeed gorgeous. She had a midnight black hair and a round face. Her rapturous blue eyes would captivate anyone.

"Oh, am I at the wrong house?" she inquired. "How can I be wrong? I come here almost every day."

"I don't know, ma'am. Who are you here to see?" asked Mahesh.

"This is Sally's house, right?" she asked politely.

"Yes, it is ma'am. I am Raju's father, Mahesh. I'm from Fiji. Today is my first day here."

"Oh!" she exclaimed. She quickly folded both her palms and greeted Mahesh in a typical Indian way. "I am Sally's aunt. My friends call me Kiran. Her mum was my eldest sister."

Mahesh also greeted her respectfully and ushered her inside. She put her small bag on the table and went straight into the kitchen. Mahesh was surprised. She acted as if she was a part of this family.

"I often come here to help Sally. Tonight she is having a party with her friends and has asked me to prepare some delicacies." She smiled at him again. Mahesh sensed a deep affection in that smile—it was the type of smile that lovers give each other. He smiled back as she had a very nice personality. She was a wizard at work. In a short period of time, she prepared several dishes and also brewed a good cup of tea for Mahesh. Whilst conversing, Mahesh came to know that she was a widow without any children. She also asked him about his family and within hours they were talking as if they had known each other for years. Mahesh watched her as she worked. Her movements were like an athlete's.

"Raju is a nice kid, but Sally has to improve herself. She is too Westernized," remarked Kiran.

Mahesh felt sorry for Kiran. After the death of her husband, she went through some very staggering times. She was treated harshly by her in-laws.

In traditional Indian society, a widow was always looked upon as a trot—a woman who brought bad luck to those near her. She could not remarry and was expected to stay indoors and wear only white clothing and no jewellery.

Kiran had been ousted from her house by her in-laws as the house was under their name. With the little government aid and insurance money she received after the demise of her husband, she managed to acquire a small room. She did petty jobs here and there, mostly as a housemaid.

A little while later, Mahek and Raju returned to the house together. Mahek was bubbling with excitement and very loquacious. She was so much like Meena. Kiran was also very fond of Mahek and hugged her warmly.

"So Dad, how was your day?" asked Raju while having tea. Mahesh looked at him and wondered how he would react if he knew about the incident in the morning—how Sally had insulted him.

He was about to say something when Sally joined them. Apparently, she had gone shopping as she carried many packages of clothing. "Hi everyone." She went to Kiran and hugged her. Before he could say anything, Mahesh caught her attention. She looked squarely at his face and all of a sudden, realization appeared to dawn on her. "Is that your dad?" she asked Raju.

"Why haven't you met Dad yet? He's been here since this morning," Raju replied.

The colour vanished from Sally's face. She looked totally shocked. Her eyes popped out in astonishment.

Maybe she realized her mistake. With a crestfallen face, she hugged Mahesh. He patted her shoulders and she did likewise.

***

A week later, an evening party was organized by Sally. Dinner tables were arranged with chairs neatly lined up. There were about ten guests, all friends of Sally's. Six young women and four men congregated around the table. As the evening passed, champagne and liquor flowed.

Kiran was asked to stay in the kitchen, and no one seemed to bother Mahesh. Sally called Mahek to sit down with them, but Mahesh could tell she did not feel comfortable. Most of the guests were now drunk and staggering.

Sally stood up. "My dear friends thank you for coming."

She could hardly stand straight. Mahesh was shocked to see her drinking like this. Raju, who used to be totally against liquor, was filling up his glass as if he had not seen liquor before in his life.

She continued. "That is my beautiful daughter," she said, pointing at Mahek. All the drunken eyes in the room were staring at her. She looked so beautiful with a thin coat of lipstick on her lips. Her innocent smiling eyes and fluttering eyelashes captivated them all. Some men were not only staring but leering at her. Mahesh could see Mahek looking very uncomfortable, but for fear of being ridiculed by her mum, she just sat there like a stone with all those hungry eyes trying to devour her.

Mahesh started getting annoyed. This was one thing that he could never bear. Women in his culture did not drink alcohol and wear revealing clothing. He, himself, was ashamed to see the way Sally dressed. Her mini dress exposed her white thighs and her semi-transparent low-cut blouse revealed her cleavage; she looked more like a whore than his own daughter-in-law.

Raju was fully drunk and just lay on the couch. The lights had been dimmed and the music was turned up to a high volume. The thumping of feet began. Amidst shouts and laughter, the living room turned into a nightclub.

Men and women grabbed each other and bundled themselves into one. Out of the corner of his eye, Mahesh saw a young man reeling and lurching, going toward Mahek. He almost sat on her lap, but Mahek stood up and he fell on the ground.

Another middle-aged man in the opposite corner took Sally in his arms and they started dancing. They were so close to each other that one would have thought they were husband and wife.

Mahesh became cautious as he realized that these drunken people were now acting like animals. Another movement distracted him. The man who fell down now stood upright and was again advancing toward Mahek. He put his hand on Mahek's shoulder and was about to grab her when a resounding slap brought him to his senses. Another slap sent him pitching face down on the floor.

Mahesh was now fuming with anger. He quickly pulled Mahek from the frenzy and was about to take her away when the lights came on. A sharp, high-pitched voice echoed through the living room.

"Stop it." It was Sally. Hardly trying to control herself she made her way to where Mahesh was.

"You old hog. This is not your father's house. How dare you touch one of my friends?"

Mahesh stood still. His face was a mask of anger. But he controlled himself.

"Sally, be calm. You don't know what this guy was trying to do," explained Mahesh politely.

"I don't want to hear it," she said. "Mahek is my daughter and I am her boss, only. Who are you to interfere in our business?"

Mahesh was shocked and wished that he had never come to this house.

Everything in this world had limitations. To be castrated and insulted in front of others and in his own son's house was nothing short of stupidity. Mahek went away crying to her room. Some of her friends tried to calm Sally, but she was fully drunk and not in her right mind.

"I do not know why Raju brought this piece of crap here from that village," she continued. "He is just a thorn in my house." She could hardly speak now.

"That stinky village and its stinky people make me sick."

She staggered badly and was about to emit more venom, when her feet gave way and she fell flat on the floor with her undergarments exposed.

For Mahesh, she was a daughter, and no father would want to see his daughter in this state. Before he could cover her up properly, Kiran appeared out of nowhere. She put a shawl on her exposed body. Meanwhile, the guests gradually eased their way out of the house. Both Raju and Sally lay on the floor, fully drunk.

It was quite late when Mahesh went to bed, after ensuring that Mahek and Kiran were safe in their rooms. Raju and Sally slept on the floor, as nothing much could be done for them. Mahesh was deep in thought. He wondered what had become of his family. There were hardly any cultural values left in the siblings. Sally hailed from such a nice and cultured family, but today she showed her real colours.

Cultured Indian ladies upheld family values in almost all families. Sally's behaviour was totally the opposite. He had only one son and he wanted both his son and daughter-in-law to live according to his family ideals. Then there was Mahek. The poor girl was totally controlled by her mum and was scared to death of her.

The clanking of utensils in the kitchen woke him up. He had slept for barely three hours. The sun was up and rays of bright sunshine pierced through the curtains, illuminating his bedroom. He opened the door slowly and made his way downstairs.

Kiran was cleaning the kitchen. Mahek also joined them and the trio did all the necessary cleaning of the kitchen and the living room.

***

It was a Tuesday. This day was meant to be a day of worship for Mahesh. Back in Fiji, he always fasted on this day and prayed. It was a day when Mahesh and his family always refrained from eating meat or drinking alcohol. He had the desire to pray. He asked Mahek whether there was a prayer room in the house.

"Grandpa, I have never seen Mum and Dad praying. Aunt Kiran told me how to pray and I have a small idol of Lord Krishna in my room where I say my prayers." Mahesh was stunned and could not believe his ears. Raju was such a devotee of God and always observed the day of Sabbath. *What has happened to him?* He wondered. How could he have changed that much?

Late in the afternoon, Raju entered the house. He was lurching and staggering as if drunk. "Mahek my baby," he said affectionately.

He took her in his arms and kissed her forehead. He was laughing and making faces. Then he turned and put his hands on Mahesh's shoulders. "How are you, Dad? Is everything okay?"

Mahesh just nodded without showing any emotion. Raju looked to be drunk but there was no smell of liquor on his breath. There was, however, a strange smell that Mahesh could not account for. Raju was in a very jovial mood. All of a sudden he started laughing again and acting crazy, as if he was overexcited or hyperactive.

About one month elapsed and Mahesh, although restless, was coming to terms with the house atmosphere. There was something weird about Raju that he could not figure out. After the house party incident, neither

Sally nor Raju said anything about it. They acted as if nothing happened.

Mahesh wanted to move back to his daughter's place but decided otherwise. He was a father and he had a moral duty toward his family, he mused.

He was more determined now than ever that he would stay there and find out more about Raju's movements.

CHAPTER TWO

Several months passed. For Raju and Sally, house parties were convened at different houses nearly every week. Mahek left them to further her final-year studies at the college. Kiran would come over and do the household chores. By this time, Mahesh was able to obtain his driver's licence and Raju gave him a 1970 Impala, a unique-looking vehicle. It was good enough for him to do his shopping and travel to nearby locations. Mahesh also started working for Raju as a salesperson on a part-time basis.

It was after eleven one chilly night when Mahesh woke up and the lights of a car in the driveway caught his attention. He casually peeped through the window. A vehicle was stopped at the house. Sally and a stranger got out of the car and stood together, talking.

Their voices could hardly be heard. After some time, the man hugged Sally and went away. Mahesh thought maybe Sally was at work and one of her friends offered to drive her home. From the half-open bedroom door, he saw Sally walking unsteadily through the house. She hit the corner of the dining room table and cursed. Mahesh knew she was drunk.

Until today, Mahesh had not said anything to Sally regarding her behaviour. He did not want to create a commotion in the house and upset the family. But if things went beyond his endurance, he would speak up. As a father, it was his duty to guide and mould them. But then, he thought, guidance should only be provided to the young ones who were often confused as to the correct path on which to tread.

Here, he was dealing with educated and mature people, the very people who ought to be paving the way for others. Still, he thought, they were his own children and their failure in life and bad reputation would be a reflection on him and his teachings. He could not sleep that night.

A host of thoughts started haunting him.

In Indian custom, women were not supposed to go out with other men, especially not to parties. If seen, the society would not only humiliate them, but would treat them as rejects.

No family would ever want their daughters or daughters-in-law to be in this predicament. They could not afford to be maligned. Females were seen as icons in every family. They epitomized reverence and respect. If they were seen with other men, it would mean a disgrace to the entire family. This type of behaviour would never be embraced by the people.

***

One evening, Mahek came to visit for the weekend. Both Sally and Raju were away. Mahesh took the opportunity to tell her and Kiran what had been happening in the house in confidence.

Mahek looked very worried and a surge of weariness clouded her face.

"Grandpa, I have been observing both Mum and Dad. I think Dad hangs around with friends who take drugs. That is why, even if he doesn't drink any liquor, he still staggers and sways like a drunkard. You might have observed that at times when he comes home he acts strangely."

Mahesh, who was quietly listening to Mahek, suddenly stood up and started pacing the floor. How could a person come into drugs if he had never even touched a cigarette? Raju had never been an advocate of cigarettes or drugs. *How could he come into this mess?* Mahek wondered. Kiran watched him quietly.

Mahek moved toward Mahesh.

"Grandpa, you look overly worried. I don't think Dad has an addiction to drugs, but continuous use could make him an addict."

"I know—I know," he said.

After a little pause, he inquired, "Okay, Kiran, you and Mahek have been here for a long time. How is their relationship? I mean, do they seem happy?"

Mahek was about to say something but Kiran signalled her to be quiet and spoke. "They are not on good terms. I am fed up with their everyday quarrelling."

Mahesh looked at Kiran. "But what has the fighting been about?" asked Mahesh.

Kiran hesitated to reply. Mahesh looked up. "Well?" he inquired.

Kiran looked away from him. She had a passive expression but her deep blue eyes showed signs of anger. She sighed and continued. "It's Sally. It is her fault. She has always treated others poorly. She even slapped me once."

Kiran was on the verge of tears. There was firmness in her voice. Mahesh frowned with disbelief. "You are her aunt—her mum's sister, just like a mother to her, and you are saying that she slapped you?"

"Yes that is exactly what I am saying. For her, relationships are for her selfish gains only. Once her wishes are fulfilled, she does not give two hoots who we are." Kiran looked annoyed. The mere reciting of the incidents of the past seemed to frustrate her, but she was determined to get it all out.

"She is so ruthless that she even swore at my family, her own mum's family. But then, what can we expect from such a nasty lady? She just brings shame on our family—she has no manners, no respect for others. Only I know what suffering I am enduring. I promised my sister who was on her death bed that I would take care of Sally and her family. Because of that, I am still sustaining the profanities she throws at me." She started panting and almost broke down.

Mahesh listened to her, bewildered, and asked, "What about Raju? Doesn't he say anything to her?"

Kiran looked worn out and irritated. "Raju!" she exclaimed. "Raju is just a tool for her. Once Raju spoke to her angrily and she raised a big commotion in the house, threatening that she would commit suicide. She is a spoiled, stubborn brat and treats him like a trash. If any one day Raju is late from work, she starts accusing him of having affairs outside. She hardly ever comes home early herself."

Mahesh sighed with weariness. He never thought things would be so bad in this house. Mahek just watched them with an innocent face.

"Raju used to pray and go to the temple every week, but they say it is a woman who makes or breaks a house," added Kiran. "There are hardly any traditional or cultural values left here. The only thing Sally knows is partying. Mahek has been raised by me and Meena. So far we have been the ones giving her the moral lessons, teaching her the ethics of life and what our deep-rooted cultures demand. She even goes to the temple with me."

Kiran breathed a sigh of relief. It was as if a big burden had slid from her shoulders. For so many years she had been yearning to share the tensions and miseries of the family that she had been carrying. Mahesh was very disturbed. Thin lines of wrinkles were visible on his forehead.

He cleared his throat and asked in a fragile voice. "Do you think it is because of these family troubles that Raju has resorted to drugs?"

Before Kiran could say anything, Mahek intervened. "Grandpa, I have learned in college that drugs are the last option before suicide for people who are mentally troubled. Drugs directly affect the mind. They can distort the user's perception of what is happening around him or her.

"As a result, the person's actions may be odd, irrational, inappropriate and even destructive. Initially, people will feel good and think their troubles are over, but gradually they will fall deeper under the spell of the drugs, until a point will come where they will find themselves on a crossroads between life and death. I think Dad has lost all hope of having a good family life and is slowly losing himself to the world of drugs."

Mahesh looked at Mahek admiringly and felt so proud of her. He wondered what all she had been through, as a daughter. As a father, he had seen the various cruel aspects of life. Mahek was still a youngster who was struggling to come to terms with it all.

She had just crossed that age group that required attention and guidance from their parents. Mothers, in particular, played a special role in guiding their kids down the correct path. Hats off to Kiran, who gave Mahek a motherly affection and who had raised her to be such a nice, cultured girl. Had it been left solely at her mum's discretion, the scenario would likely have been very different.

Sally persistently came home late under the influence of liquor. When Mahesh saw this happening almost every day, he summoned Raju. "Raju, there is something very important that I think you need to know."

Raju, half-drunk, slid onto the sofa beside his dad. He looked at Mahesh inquiringly.

"It is Sally," Mahesh continued.

Raju scowled and said, "What about her?"

"I think you ought to be more vigilant about her activities. The way she behaves and parties at night does not look good. I have raised you according to our traditions and beliefs, and . . ."

Raju cut him off abruptly. "Oh, Dad. Same story again. What did she do?" he asked.

Mahesh frowned. "What did she do?" he repeated. "Raju, as a good husband, it is your duty to ensure that the respect and dignity of the family is maintained at all times. Sally comes home late with other men and she is often seen drunk."

Raju burst into laughter. He apparently took this as a joke.

"So what, Dad? This is not Fiji. This is Czekeland. Both men and women socialize. I don't see anything wrong with that."

Mahesh glared at him in disbelief. He wondered how a man could be so unperturbed. Was this the same Raju he nurtured and brought up? Frustrated, he walked away.

Raju wore a lopsided smile and said, “Don’t worry, Dad. I will take care of things.” Without saying anything else, Mahesh banged his bedroom door shut.

***

It was early in the morning that running footsteps awakened him. Someone burst into his bedroom. Before he could even rise from the bed, a sharp, piercing voice rang out. “You old man! Do you want to live here or shall we kick you out?”

Sally was in a frenzied mood. Her face was a mask of uncontrollable rage. Her curled lips were lined with froth. She snarled at Mahesh.

Mahesh tried to calm her down. “Hold on, Sally. Hold on. What is the problem?”

“You are the problem,” Sally retorted. “We gave you a place to live and even found a part-time job for you. You eat and sleep here, yet you have the gall to go against me.” She was seething. Her red dyed hair was unruly and wet with sweat. Her long, painted fingernails shone as if she was holding a couple of steel knives. Her skin was pallid and there were dark smudges under her eyes. It looked as if she had not slept the entire night. Her savage eyes glowed like a charcoal.

Mahesh remained calm and politely said, “Sally, please listen to me. If you have problems, we can always talk.”

She looked even more angry and railed at him. “There is nothing more to talk about. You complained to Raju that I am not a good wife—you told him that I go out with other men. How dare you incite him against me!”

Mahesh cut in. “No, that is not true. I just asked him why you always come home late and drunk. I . . .” He could not complete what he wanted to say.

Sally recoiled. “You filthy man! You are here like a beggar. If you have to make snide comments, go and make them to your low-down daughter.”

Mahesh could take no more as she called his daughter “low-down” when everybody knew that she was very cultured and decent. He became furious, and, without thinking, he lunged toward Sally. He was about to slap her when Kiran intercepted.

“Please don’t,” she snapped. She was in the kitchen and the early morning commotion could not go unnoticed by her.

Her voice had that ring of authority that elders had when they spoke to their children. Mahesh stopped where he was and all of a sudden realized the grave mistake he was about to commit.

Kiran turned to Sally. “Please, Sally. That is enough.” She held Sally and ushered her outside the room. But Sally freed herself and leaped toward Mahesh. She screamed, “Listen, you dirty face—from the time you arrived, I’ve hardly had any peace or privacy in this house, and today you dared to raise your hand against me." She cried, "You will pay for this!" and stomped her way out.

Kiran tried to explain to the equally fuming Mahesh not to ever raise his hand against a female, as they had many rights in Western countries. Most women were disciplined and decent, but there were some who abused those rights of freedom.

Gradually, Mahesh cooled down and wondered why he could not control his anger today. This was the first time in his life that he had given in to the fangs of anger. Had Kiran not been there, the consequences of his actions could have been worse.

He was still brooding over his actions, when Raju angrily stormed into his bedroom. He also appeared very angry and annoyed and jabbed his fingers almost into Mahesh's eyes.

"Dad, what is wrong with you? How dare you assault Sally?" He was enraged and shaking with anger.

"I did not assault her, Raju. I just expressed my anger with her." Mahesh replied calmly.

"From now on, you better mind your own damn business. Do not try to lecture us or else." With that, he walked away, slamming the door.

Mahesh felt dazed. He could not digest the fact that his son, Raju, would treat him that way. Today he saw a new Raju—the very son who used to be an icon back in the village. How could he be so disrespectful?

He had not yet had his breakfast when the doorbell rang. Kiran opened the door to find two uniformed cops.

They brushed her aside and moved into the house. Upon seeing Mahesh, they rushed toward him.

"Are you Mahesh?" one of the cops asked. He nodded. Immediately, one of them held his arms and twisted them. Mahesh did not resist but cried in pain. The other cop quickly handcuffed him. Both his hands tied behind him, he was dragged outside and dumped into the police vehicle. Before Kiran could speak, they took him away.

Kiran, her eyes wide and mouth open, just looked helpless.

They took him to the police station, and, after passing a series of doorways, locked him in a cell, without asking any questions. It was fairly dark inside, but Mahesh could make out a small table and a chair resting in the corner. There were no windows. He sat down in a corner and massaged his wrists where the handcuffs had been secured. He could see bloodstains on his wrists in the semi-darkness.

He tried to close his eyes but could not as he was famished. He had not eaten anything that morning. The floor was cold and he could feel shivers running through his body. A surge of emotion gripped him. He could not forget how his son had treated him today. He suddenly realized how lonely he had become by coming to a foreign land. Tears started rolling down his cheeks.

He put his head on his knees and started sobbing. Feeling rejected and so helpless, he could not control his tears. He cried and cried. Half-dazed, he slowly slipped into a slumber.

***

He saw Curly very clearly. She wore a long white gown and her beautiful smiling face gave her added glamour. Her unfaltering gaze rested on Mahesh. She opened her arms as if calling him. He tried to go near her but felt something holding him back. His second attempt was not futile. He felt himself come free and he thrust himself toward Curly, only to find himself lying face down on the floor. It was a dream. This was not the first time he'd seen Curly in his dreams. Whenever he was in a grave situation, he would see her. These sightings always boosted his morale.

Mahesh stood up and looked out the cell door. A clock in the hallway showed 4:10. "Oh my God, the day has almost passed," he muttered to himself.

His gaze shifted to the long hallway and he could make out a thin ray of sunlight illuminating the area. He wondered how long he would be kept there. Was this his punishment for talking back to a lady? Inwardly, he cursed himself for not restraining himself and his emotions. His thoughts went from one place to another just like a bird flitting from one branch to the next. He sat down on the old chair, grimacing when a series of thudding steps stopped at his cell door.

It was a female cop this time. She spoke politely and summoned Mahesh to the front desk. Mahesh was guided out of the cell and he made his way down the hallway to the front desk. He blinked once or twice to get accustomed to the bright sunlight that pierced through the glass windows of the police station.

To his surprise, he saw Raju with Kiran. Raju came toward him and embraced his dad affectionately. "I am really sorry, Dad." He started crying like a small child. "It was not my fault. I had no idea that Sally would call the cops. Please, Dad, I am indeed sorry."

Before Mahesh could say anything, Raju kneeled down and touched Mahesh's feet. He stayed there for some time, washing his dad's feet with his tears before Mahesh picked him up and passionately embraced him.

"It's okay, my son. I understand." He wiped the tears from Raju's cheeks and felt happy that at last he got his Raju back.

Later, he learned that both Kiran and Raju had given a written statement to the police that the allegations of assault against Mahesh were false—that they were present at the scene and at no point did Mahesh touch Sally. Raju took them to a cafeteria to have a light meal before he took them to the hospital. Upon inquiry, it was revealed that Meena had given birth to a baby boy. That was a great piece of news for Mahesh. He was indeed happy and thought how destiny played its game. An hour before, he was crying as if no one in this world cared for him. Now, within a short interval, he was beaming with happiness.

***

The next day saw him back at the temple he had been frequenting. Due to his active participation in religious activities, he was now the vice president of the temple.

His friends and colleagues greeted him as usual, but their looks appeared to say something else. In one of the corners, he overheard two women talking. "Do you know, sister? This person was in a cell because he hit his daughter-in-law." The other responded by saying, "Shhh, he's coming." They thought Mahesh did not hear anything, but he did. These rumors were twisted and exaggerated to such an extent that it became news for every Fijian household in the area. As soon as he went out, one of his friends accosted him. "Mahesh, what happened? There are lots of stories circulating about you. How can a person like you do this?"

"Do what?" Mahesh inquired.

"People are saying that you made sexual advances toward your own daughter-in-law and that is why you were confined to the cell."

Mahesh was dumbfounded. His eyes bulged in anger. This was a lie being propagated by some influential members of the community who wanted to see him removed from his post. He was about to smash the face of that person.

With clenched wrists, he forced himself to retain control. He forced his *anger* and *frustration* away to keep his *eyes* from flashing amber. Without responding, he just walked away from there.

In another corner there stood several men, who, all of a sudden, quietened when they saw him. Obviously, they were gossiping about him. Anywhere he went,people eyed him with hatred and disgust. He knew that the area was now buzzing with the false allegation someone had propagated.

The type of allegations only low-down and cheap people made. Mahesh gauged the politics of the temple committee and warned himself to be cautious. He went home in deep thought. *What has happened to our people?* He wondered. Temples were meant to be places of worship, where people not only prayed but exchanged ideas and forged better relationships. They were the places where humane values were respected.

But today he had seen a completely different side to the temple he had served since his arrival in the country. The nasty chit-chat and gossiping about others appeared to be the only agenda. In lieu of having talks to make religious and cultural values more cohesive, people were eager to castrate and malign others.

***

The living room was delicately decorated. Dazzling and elegant chandeliers illuminated the surroundings. This was the sixth-day ritual gathering most people observed when there was a newborn in the family. Som and Meena invited their friends and relatives. Most of the men were dressed in a bow ties and vests whilst others attired themselves in suits. Women mostly wore floor-length formal gowns. Some were draped in bright-coloured Indian *saris* or *saris* with *choli* tops. The elegance of their glimmering clothing and dazzling jewellery added charm to the atmosphere. Excitement, cheers and laughter filled the room amidst the clinking of glasses. Swarms of children ran through the house as bubbles floated in the air and balloons drifted aimlessly among discarded wrapping paper.

Multi-coloured banners were draped across the top of each door. A stack of unopened presents stood in the corner of the room, wrapped in smooth, shiny wrapping paper. A silk bow had been carefully tied around each parcel. Guests loomed over the table, which was filled with food and drinks. They grabbed at sandwiches and filled their mouths with Indian sweets. A sweet melody drifted over the enchanted atmosphere.

Mahesh wore a simple long-sleeved green shirt with white pants that caught the attention of several people. He had added a wee bit of dye to the grey areas of his hair and was looking very handsome. He was there with Mahek and Kiran. As usual, Mahek was wearing a simple, long, shiny dress but it was her natural beauty and charm that garnered second looks from men.

Kiran appeared shy and timid. She had put on an old blue *sari* and wore a captivating smile. She wore little facial makeup. Her personality and graceful walk with downcast eyes depicted the virtues of a typical Indian woman.

Meena was very pleased to see them. She was also clad in a typical Indian *sari*. The baby boy in her lap bore a real semblance to Mahesh, the proud grandpa. He was jubilant when he got to hold the baby in his arms amidst cheers from the guests. Som grabbed Meena forcefully and started dancing. Mahek also joined them. The thumping of feet and graceful moves of the guests ensued.

All of a sudden, the dancing came to standstill when a sharp, rattling voice cut through the air. “What is all this going on here?”

All eyes turned toward the speaker. It was none other than the same frail old woman that Mahesh had encountered on his first day here.

It was Som’s mother. She was neatly dressed in white robes and nicely styled grey hair. All this time, she had chosen to remain inconspicuous, sitting in a corner that gave a clear view of the room. Although in a wheelchair, her voice commanded authority. Som edged his way toward his mum. She looked at him inquiringly.

“Mum, it’s okay. We are just enjoying ourselves. Please don’t worry.”

She frowned. “What kind of enjoyment is this? I am now blessed with a grandchild and we should do all the rituals that we have always done.” She looked annoyed and moved toward Meena.

Meena could not meet her unfaltering stare. She no doubt realized now that there should have been prayers and some old traditional songs before the actual partying began. “Mum you are correct. I did call the folk singers and wanted to carry out the sixth-day ritual, but Som did not see that as necessary.”

She stopped, bracing for a backlash. But the old mum sat motionless, and all of a sudden she started singing an old traditional folk song. She took the baby on her lap and slowly moved in between the crowd. All eyes were fixed upon this granny, whose face now shone like a marble stone. She looked happy and proud. The other guests clapped and joined her. Granny stopped and took out a package. It held a gold chain which she put around the neck of the baby. She was on the verge of tears and slowly kissed her grandson on his forehead. With a small smile, she faced the guests again.

"My dear sons and daughters." She cleared her throat. "It is so nice to see you all here. I know most of you are from our beloved Fiji, and I feel that I am back in Nadi, my hometown. I was thirty years old when I came here. At that time, very few people from Fiji were here. I made many white friends and often went out with them to places. There was never a time when I did anything that would have tarnished my beliefs and religion.

"You are in the Western world, so sophisticated and advanced. You should not only value your cultures, but give equal respect to the beliefs of others. That does not mean that you also need to observe and execute what they are practising."

She looked around as if looking for someone. There was a pin-drop silence. All eyes were focused on her. Suddenly she fixed her gaze at a distance. All eyes turned toward the centre of her gaze.

Sally and Raju were making their way in. Raju was casually dressed and was staggering. He appeared drunk. Sally caught everyone's attention. She looked very pretty and alluring. Curls of dyed black hair hung loosely from her head, almost covering her face. A mini dress and low-cut blouse exposed her body. Some women stared at her with envy whilst others giggled. The clothing Sally wore would never be accepted by the society in which they lived. Older men leered at her. The men who were half drunk ogled her like hungry wolves.

Some of Mahesh's friends looked at Sally and then at him. Mahesh knew what was going on in their minds. He was very much embarrassed and ashamed. As a leader in the community, he used to advise others on the need to dress respectably. Women in his culture were held in high esteem and afforded much respect. His own daughter-in-law in this condition was definitely a slap in his face.

Oblivious of the way they were looking at her, Sally decently greeted everyone and presented Meena with a gift while Raju curled himself into a sofa. Som's mum frowned at Sally disapprovingly. Her keen old eyes sized her up. Mahesh just hoped that the old woman wouldn't say anything to Sally or there would be chaos. Much to Mahesh' relief, she coughed twice and carried on, her voice husky but sharp.

"Always maintain your social values with special attention to your culture and religion. What you wear, how you wear it, how you treat others, how you tread in all aspects of life and your attitude, all together contribute to your overall identity. A person who cannot maintain his heritage in such a beautiful country as this will always be seen as a failure and will never command respect from anyone." Everyone in the hall nodded in agreement. Sally was open-mouthed, no doubt having sensed that the old woman was directing the comments at her. The old woman had a good look at her, and, before turning away, she said in the same raspy voice, "Please go on with the celebrations."

She slowly took her wheelchair to the corner where she had sat earlier. The celebrations started again. Mahesh looked at Kiran who sat alone in the other corner. He went over to her and was about to say something when Mahek came from behind.

"Grandpa," she said.

Mahesh turned around. Mahek had company. A young man with a fair complexion and frizzy hair smiled at him.

"Grandpa, this is Doctor Sam Naivalu." Mahesh was flabbergasted. How did this white man have a Fijian surname? Both shook hands warmly.

"How are you, Mr. Sam Naivalu?" asked Mahesh.

Sam again threw him a wide smile. "I am good, sir. Thank you." He flashed a wide grin. Sam was a tall, handsome young man clad in an expensive blue suit that gave him the look of a pilot. He had an oval face with a thin black moustache above his thin pink lips. Clad in his suave blue suit and red tie, he certainly attracted a lot of attention—especially from the women.

"Grandpa, Sam has just graduated and is now a full-time doctor. He is specialized in the field of psychiatry." Mahek beamed with happiness.

"Oh, congratulations, Mr. Sam. So nice to see you. Please enjoy the evening."

Sam thanked him and took Mahek back to the dance floor. Mahesh watched them for some time.

It was close to midnight when the party ended. Before going to sleep, Mahesh paced around his bedroom in deep thought. He was very much concerned with the deteriorating habits of both Sally and Raju. As a father, he would be deemed responsible for the failures of his children. He considered various options to embrace, but could not make a firm decision. One thing was clear: he would not leave this house until Sally and Raju were on the path he desired for them. He could not force them to adhere to the Indian way of living, but by being there he would at least be able to make some difference in their lives. Tonight, the address Som's mother gave still ricocheted through his mind. These were the very ideals that he embraced and preached. He thought the old woman was a nasty piece of work, but today he realized she was full of morals. Maybe because of her archaic beliefs in traditions and practices, she seemed out of place. But no, she only had to accept that change was inevitable. To bring cultural values to a different country, one had to be flexible. Depending on circumstances, surroundings and resources, one had to make modifications.

Her biggest drawback was the discriminatory views she had toward human beings. Being born into a priestly family did not mean a person had the virtues of an upper-caste group of people. It was not about where one was born, or which family one was born into. It was not about the financial status or popularity of a person—it was one's deeds that declared a person to be supreme or a low life.

He must have dozed for all of five minutes when an incessant thudding and banging in the vicinity startled him. He lay motionless, listening. Again, a scraping sound followed by a big *thud* made him fully awake. *What could it be?* He wondered. A loud cry of pain sounded. Then there was silence for some time. Mahesh wiped drops of sweat from his forehead. Again, a longer wave of thudding reverberated. He heard running footsteps. Quickly, he opened his bedroom door, and the scene that met his eyes almost took the last breath out of him.

CHAPTER THREE

It was Raju, who had somehow crawled from his bedroom and was now slithering on the hallway floor. Frothy saliva was smeared all over his face. He tried to stand up but could not. His attempt to sit upright apparently caused him acute pain. This made him cry. Kiran was the first one at his side. She tried to lift him but could not. Mahesh ran and gave her a helping hand. After several attempts they managed to make him sit in an upright position. He was dazed and his face looked swollen. Tears flowed from his red eyes. Mahesh carefully laid him onto his lap and tried to soothe him. A series of hiccups was followed by vomiting. Mahek suddenly came running from her bedroom.

"What's wrong with Dad?" she cried. She appeared very scared. "Grand pa, is he okay? Why is he vomiting?"

Kiran tried to soothe Mahek, wiping her tears. "He is okay, my dear."

Mahesh asked Kiran to wake Sally up. Raju closed his eyes. He was not writhing in pain anymore. Still lying on Mahesh's lap, he had apparently slid into unconsciousness.

"Raju . . . Raju." He shook him hard and tried to wake him up but there was no response. Mahek also shook her dad, hard.

"Dad . . . Dad . . . wake up, Dad." She again started sobbing. Mahesh saw that Raju's face was starting to turn blue. Kiran came back running.

"She is deeply asleep. I think she had one too many last night."

"It's okay. We should take him to the hospital now."

"Grandpa, shall I call the ambulance? He won't be able to walk and in this state he is too heavy for you to lift alone."

"No, I think I will manage." He laid him there and quickly changed into clothing that was more presentable. Then Mahesh deftly picked Raju up as if he was lifting a big bag of flour. He hoisted him on his shoulders and started descending the stairs. Mahek and Kiran could not believe their eyes. They all rushed outside. With Mahek in the driver's seat, they rushed to the hospital.

The hospital was busy even at that hour. Raju was quickly taken into a room. They were all asked to stay outside, although Mahesh insisted on going in. But the doctor disallowed it and assured him that everything would be all right.

They waited outside for more than two hours. Mahesh impatiently started pacing the floor. He asked Mahek and Kiran to leave and get some rest, but they would not budge. After a while, the doctor summoned Mahesh inside and said, "He took a high dosage of drugs last night. It is good that you brought him here in time." Mahesh saw Raju sleeping peacefully. The bluish colour of his face had vanished.

"We have given him some medication and he should be fine within an hour or so."

Mahesh came out relieved and shared the good news with Mahek and Kiran. They left, as Mahek was to return to college in the morning. Shortly afterwards, before the day broke, Mahesh saw Sally walking toward him.

"Hi Dad. I'm sorry. Mahek called me early in the morning and told me about Raju. I guess I was in a very deep sleep when all this happened." She glanced at Mahesh who was sitting in a chair, weary and motionless.

"How is Raju now?" She was panting and looked worried.

Mahesh beckoned her to the room Raju was in. After a while, she came out, crestfallen, and again apologized to Mahesh. There was a look of regret and, maybe, repentance on her face.

"Dad, let's go home. Raju is resting now. You should also get some rest." Mahesh gave her a queer look but decided that was a good idea. On the way home, both were silent, and Mahesh wondered what kind of woman Sally was. She was acting as if nothing had happened between them. How could she face him after insulting him? He was like a father to her. She had behaved in a very unruly manner and now she was driving him home.

***

A week later, Raju was back on his feet but there were no changes in his habits.

He was often seen to be under the influence of drugs. Mahesh did not know what to do. As a father, he wanted him to stay away from drugs completely. He knew it would not be an easy task, but he couldn't lose hope. Some of his friends at the temple advised him to take Raju to a specialist, whilst others told him about an Indian guy who had divine powers. This person could invoke powers by which all evil spirits would vanish. Mahesh had heard a lot about these witch doctors, most of whom were fakes and cheaters. He waited for almost one month, all the time thinking that Raju would be okay with the medications he was taking.

Unfortunately, his condition was getting worse. He often vomited and several times, he was spotted on the floor beside his bed. It appeared that during sleep, he often fell out of bed without waking up. Sally shared the same bed, but due to her excessive alcohol intake, she had no idea what transpired in her own bedroom.

Mahesh did not see any other option. He decided to seek out the services of a witch doctor. His close friend, Andrew, offered to take him to a witch doctor by the name of Baba Dhilu. He was a popular doctor among the Fijian community and several people vouched for his credibility. Andrew told Mahesh that one parent had lost all hope for their child, who had acute cancer. Baba's herbal medicines had acted like a miracle. Within a week, the boy was seen running around. In another case, medical doctors had lost all hope of saving the life of a mother who gave birth to twins. The husband sought Baba's services and she recovered in no time.

"Does he charge for his services?" inquired Mahesh.

Andrew just waved him off. "Don't worry about the cost. Life is more important than money. The only problem we may face is reaching the place."

"Why, what is the problem?" Mahesh was getting curious.

"The problem we have is how to get there. I have his contacts. But he does not operate from his home." Andrew pointed to the distant mountain range.

"Down there in the caves of the Stony Mountains is his lair from where he operates." Andrew chuckled. "Don't worry, I will call him and schedule an appointment. The only thing we need now is a four-wheel-drive truck or jeep because of the rough terrain we will encounter."

***

A week later, on a chilly morning, Mahesh picked Andrew up and the duo headed for the dreaded thick jungle. After about two hours of driving, the road led them into the hills where the vegetation was sparse. After more driving, they were suddenly surrounded by big trees and dense jungle. The foliage made a crackling sound as the vehicle proceeded through it. Meandering their way through the dark jungle, they finally came to a small track that was muddy and wet. Andrew asked Mahesh to park the vehicle as the track ahead was not meant for commuters.

With a big knife in his hand, Andrew led the way down the muddy track. It zigzagged around the huge tree trunks. The wet mud clung to their shoes. The smell of mud and rotting plants made them hold their noses from time to time. Myriads of insects clustered on dead animals they saw here and there. The warbling of various species of birds and strange animal sounds gave Mahesh an eerie feeling. The sun was up, but due to the tall trees shrouded by the thick foliage, it was fairly dark. After about an hour of trudging down the path, they managed to reach a small clearing. In a distant they could see a small cave.

"That's it!" Andrew exclaimed. "That cave there leads into the place where Baba practices his witchcraft. I will go first to make sure that he is there. You just wait here, my friend. I will be back in no time."

Before Mahesh could open his mouth, he was on his way. Mahesh watched him go. After a while, he could only see a tiny figure in the distance. It soon faded. With nothing to do, Mahesh sat on an outcropping and waited for his return.

It did not take long for Andrew to return. He guided Mahesh along a bushy track into the cave. Surprisingly, the cave was not at all dark. Streams of sunlight could be seen. It appeared that the ceiling of the cave had multiple cracks.

The place gave Mahesh a weird feeling. When they reached the small shack built into the cave, Andrew signalled Mahesh to enter. The inside was lighted by several candles in pots.

A brass plate held burning camphor, and the fragrance of incense sticks filled the atmosphere. An old man clad in yellow robes sat beside the doorway, apparently in deep meditation. On top of the doorframe was a piece of wood on which was written "Baba Dhilu." This was the person he had come to see. He folded both his hands in greeting, but Baba still had his eyes closed.

The witch doctor had a long white beard and his hair resembled that of an old woman—long and plaited, and tied in a knot.

Without opening his eyes, Baba spoke. "My son, you don't have to say anything. You are facing lot of problems in this country. Your daughter-in-law has gone astray. Your son is addicted to drugs. You are pretty much alone, not knowing what to do."

The voice sounded so familiar. He felt as if he had heard that voice somewhere before, but he was so bewildered by what Baba said that he did not give it a second thought.

Mahesh was not only dumbfounded but baffled, as well. He could feel drops of sweat trickling down his cheeks. He just did not know what to say. How could a stranger know so much about his family? *This Baba must really possess divine powers,* he mused.

"Your problems will be gone in one month. Don't you worry, son. There are some ingredients that you need to bring with you at any cost. Once that is done, I will invoke my powers to ward off the evil spirits that are troubling your family."

Mahesh was overwhelmed. He could not control his happiness.

"Thank you so much, Baba. Once Raju gets well, I will gift you well."

He bent down and touched his feet.

Baba than gave Mahesh a piece of paper on which several items were listed.

"Please, liaise with Andrew if you have any difficulties. He is my ardent devotee."

"Thank you, Baba. Thank you so much."

Mahesh again kneeled before Baba to receive his blessing and backed out of the shack. On the way back, he read through the list, but he couldn't interpret the items listed. The names sounded so strange. He turned to Andrew for help.

"Do not worry, my friend. I will take care of things. There are some things that I have to have shipped from India. The rest, I can buy. Five hundred dollars should suffice."

Mahesh felt relieved and quickly opened his wallet. He plucked a couple of notes and handed them to Andrew.

"Andrew, there are only three hundred dollars here. I owe you another two hundred. I will give you the balance when we reach home."

"No problem, my friend," Andrew said. A week later, Andrew brought him herbal medications in a bottle and some ashes.

Kiran was given the responsibility to ensure that Raju consumed these with his usual diet. Two months elapsed, and, with the medications exhausted, Raju still did not show any signs of improvement. Mahesh approached Andrew several times but he appeared to ignore him now.

He just hoped that his going to that Baba was not a farce—he had spent so much money. But then, he thought, Baba had that godly power. Without his telling him anything, he had known so much about him.

***

Mahek was back home for the mid-term break. Mahesh was so pleased to see her. While having dinner, Mahesh briefed Mahek and Kiran on his going to see Baba and spending over five hundred dollars, as well as the divine powers Baba had displayed and the cave he practised in, beyond the thick jungle.

Kiran looked thoughtful and after the meal, while washing dishes, she murmured to Mahek. "I think your grandpa has been cheated."

"What?" exclaimed Mahek.

"I am not positive," continued Kiran, "but there are reports of a scam going on in which some influential people are involved." Mahek looked at Kiran with concerned eyes, but remained silent.

"We should tell Grandpa," said Mahek.

"No . . . no," Kiran said. "There is nothing concrete. I cannot prove that I am right. If we tell Mahesh now, he will become more worried. Let us find out for sure first—I will find the article that ran last week in the newspaper."

Mahek looked at Kiran with affection. She was more a mother to her than her real mother.

"I have an idea, Aunty," Mahek responded. "Do you remember that young man who was with me at the party?"

"You mean that doctor with a Fijian surname?" asked Kiran.

"Yeah, Doctor Sam, Aunty. He has connections with almost all the cops and news media, because he used to work for the media and then he was assigned research work with the police force. I will find out from him first, then we will see," assured Mahek.

In the meantime, the worries Mahesh had about his son doubled. His tense face and worried expression spoke volumes. Later that week, Mahek came home with Doctor Sam. They spoke to Mahesh at length. He cautioned him against the witch doctors there. After listening to what actually transpired with Mahesh, Doctor Sam said, "Uncle, I think you ought to report this to the police. At least you know Andrew, the person who took you there. Cops can find out from him the credibility of this so-called 'Baba.'"

He stood up to leave, but after a little pause, he looked at the worried face of Mahesh and said, "Uncle, please do not worry. From now onwards I will treat Raju. I have dealt with worse cases in the past. This one should not be a problem." He picked up his briefcase, and, after bidding goodbye, to Mahek went out. Mahesh watched him leave with a feeling of gratitude. He felt relieved. He wasted no time in reporting the incident to the cops, as advised by Doctor Sam.

***

Grey clouds hung over the temple, which was also known as Bhakti Place. They could be seen rolling and playing hide-and-seek among themselves. It looked as if it would rain. A cool breeze from the western side of the mountains sent chills through the hundreds of people gathered at the temple. It was the day of the most popular event of the year, the "Talent Quest."

The temple authorities organized this oratory contest to not only test the skills of the young people, but also to get ideas from the students on various topics. The yearly contest always attracted hundreds of spectators, with contestants ranging from ten-year-olds to those in their fifties. The topics chosen were typically ones that dealt with the activities and ideals of the temple.

This morning, about three hundred people—including men, women and children—mingled with each other in anticipation of a great speaking contest. Women in dark-coloured *saris* and men in their usual long-sleeved shirts and long pants waited patiently for the contest to begin. Busloads of college students could be seen disembarking and gathering in the Bhakti arena.

The dignitaries consisted of the mayor of the cityMr. Charles Chambers; the area MLA, Gurbuksh Singh; and the chief of police, Gerry. The temple president, Mr. Atma Maharaj, accompanied by other officials, lined up in front of the seats on the stage. Mahesh, who was still the vice president was not invited or asked to join them on the stage. This could be attributed to the false rumours about Mahesh that poisoned the minds of the community. Also, Mahesh posed a challenge to Atma for the position of the presidency. There were rumours that Mahesh would be seeking a bid for presidency that year.

Atma, the current president, could not afford to lose this election, as he was eyeing to contest the city elections later that year. He was a shrewd and successful businessman and was very influential throughout the country. It was evident that he was hell-bent on defaming Mahesh so that public would not vote for him.

Mahesh, along with Kiran and Raju, sat in one corner of Bhakti Place, where several chairs were set out for the occasion.

It was a big day for them, especially Mahek. The day she would make her first speech in front of a large crowd.

The chief guest would speak on a topic no one knew. The contestants would need to listen, analyze and then respond to the issues raised by the topic.

The president, Atma, was not a fluent speaker; therefore, the acting president took care of the formalities of welcoming the crowd and making introductions. Atma's son, Krit Maharaj, was one of the best orators in the area and was pegged to be the winner of this year's contest.

One by one, the participants were introduced and the volley of cheers that followed indicated the number of supporters they had. Mahek was the tenth one called. Only a light clapping could be heard since only ten of her friends from the college could come support her.

The chief guest spoke on the need to have a good management team for any social, religious or cultural group, in order to steer people in the correct direction. He also touched on issues related to immigrants—their rights and obligations. With a view to make the country a better place, he invited the contestants to make their statements.

Almost all the speakers were very impressive in their presentations. Most of them touched on the need for immigrants to have more religious rights. The crowd cheered and clapped whenever these views were expressed.

Atma's son, Krit Maharaj, appeared to be the star speaker. He expressed the need to have influential people and elites at the head of any organization. On the immigration issue, Krit spoke boldly and asked people to organize marches and protests if their demands were not met. He more or less incited the audience to be active if they wanted to achieve anything in this world. He was very fluent. The crowd went wild listening to him. Mahesh saw the young man's dad, Atma Maharaj, sitting pompously amidst the officials. Atma gave a slight, sneering smile when he saw Mahesh gazing at him. He raised his hands for the crowd to calm down. All eyes were now upon Mahek, the lone girl in the competition, who did not attract much applause from the audience. Mahesh could feel the thumping of his heartbeat. He was not scared but a bit nervous to see his granddaughter take the stage. Mahek looked very confident.

"Ladies and gentlemen, I have come here today, not to win the contest, but to win the hearts of the people. Mr. Chairman, sir, I do not agree with what the other speakers have said. I am not one of those who condone 'Yes, Boss' policies—in other words, blindly following what your leader says."

A few claps from the audience ensued. Mahek today looked very poised and determined—Mahesh had never seen her look like this before.

"As far as organizations are concerned," she continued after a short pause, "for any organization to prosper, we not only need leaders elected based on their financial or social status, we also need people who are visionary, diligent, experienced and, above all, educated. To say that only capitalists or popular people should be the heads of organizations is not only idiotic, but irresponsible. There are so many duds who have lots of money. Does that mean that they should be given the position of president in an organization? Our biggest failure these days is putting people in positions they do not deserve. Some people join organizations just to attain power and to further their selfish gains."

She paused, and, after looking at the president, Atma, she added, "We do not need bullies or fakers at the helm of any organization."

This was followed by some cheering and clapping. Mahesh saw Atma's face turn red. Mahesh, who had been feeling a bit downtrodden, now sat up with pride. He stared back at the leering president. Raju, who had been expressionless until now, also appeared to take interest in what his daughter was saying. Friends of Mahek who had been sitting grim-faced now stood up and walked near the stage—their confidence in their friend appeared to be returning.

"All of my learned colleagues that spoke before me were repetitive on immigration issues. Ladies and gentlemen, let us not forget that we come from various countries with our own sets of ideals and beliefs. Did this country call us?"

She looked left and right and, smiling, continued, "No, it didn't. We came here of our own will—to better our futures and to have a better lifestyle than before we all came here.

"Instead of demanding things from the government, don't you think it would be wise for us to respectfully request our needs?

"We should be thankful that we enjoy most of the same provisions that are available to the citizens here. Those who embrace the idea of protest marches and demonstrations no doubt have other ulterior motives.

"To instigate people against the country we call our home is a clear indication of the short-sightedness some of our friends here have. Only leaders who are illiterate and who lack the vision to lead will resort to such tactics."

"Boo . . . boo . . . boo . . ."

Mahek paused to look out into the audience. There was a slight disturbance in the crowd. A couple of people in the crowd were giving her the finger and booing. Mahek did not get disheartened but shifted her gaze to the other corner.

"My dear friends, I am just giving you an example. We go to the house of a stranger who is good enough to give us a decent place to live in. Once we are a bit established, we demand to have a place of worship in his house; we demand that the homeowner change the colour of the house; we demand that the vegetarian homeowner allow us to cook meat there . . . Just think which homeowner would ever want to give us shelter, if we adopt such attitudes. We will be kicked out in no time. We have come here from different backgrounds and faiths.

"To stimulate goodwill and prosperity, a good leader will always tell you to modify and merge gradually into the system. Do not impose but revere, treasure and respect whatever is available. Most of our immigrants have a high calibre and they are diligent, as well. When they come to a new place, they need guidance, and if we have able and visionary leaders in religious and social entities, they will be steered in the correct directions. However, if capitalists or bullies sit at the head table, they often get lost. This is why, for immigrants, my only message to you is to take another look at your organizational heads—if you need to, change them. Bring in people who can effectively foster peace and harmony, not only in the community but in the country, as well. Thank you."

Cheers echoed. The crowd went into a frenzy. Amidst the clapping and cheers, the loud booing again erupted. It was apparent that most of the audience did not like the views expressed by Mahek. The president, Atma, and his devotees apparently could not digest what Mahek said in her speech. Their sour faces and ugly mood said a lot.

Out of the corner of his eye, Mahesh suddenly caught a glimpse of Sally. An old man was arguing with her. There were several other people behind him talking loudly. Many of the people sitting in the front rows could be seen chatting frantically.

Mahesh found his heart sinking and he knew beyond a doubt that Mahek was losing today. He was content, however, that she put up a brilliant performance. Raju also looked distressed. The chairman of the panel of judges started summarizing the views presented by the orators. The air was tense. The grey clouds above now started rolling angrily. The intensity of the westerly breeze increased, whipping the yellow flag that was at full mast.

Light raindrops could be felt. Mahesh knew that it would be pouring soon. He escorted Kiran out of the melee and signalled Raju to join them. Sally also followed them.

"Ladies and gentlemen," the speakers boomed.

"Today all the speakers spoke brilliantly. One of the best speakers in the contest Krit Maharaj put up a very impressive performance like he has been doing in the previous years.

He could say no more. The deafening applause shook Bhakti Place as if thunder was rolling through it. The cheers and applause went on for some time. It was with great difficulty that the chairman managed to contain the wild crowd.

"But . . . but . . ." He paused for a moment. There was a sudden silence that encompassed the atmosphere. A silence similar to the one you see before a storm. President Atma, who was on the stage hugging the other officials in happiness, all of a sudden stood motionless.

"But the winner of this contest is young Mahek Prasad." Again the Bhakti Place echoed with applause, but this time the cheers came from a different faction of audience, who until now had been quiet. Mahesh ran toward the stage, followed by Kiran, Raju and Sally. Before Mahek could come forward and take her trophy, they hugged her passionately. She cried in happiness and was so happy to see them. A jagged bolt of lightning flashed in the sky, followed by a roaring thunder clap. The torrential downpour and everyone was drenched to the skin before they could get into their cars.

"This is a blessing for my Mahek," uttered Mahesh, smiling as their car moved toward sweet home.

CHAPTER FOUR

Mahesh had five more months to stay in Czekeland, as his visa would expire soon. The AGM for the temple would be held soon. No one in the temple committee knew that he had a temporary visa to stay. His plan was to topple the current president, who was ruthless and not at all active. Atma was more of a puppet to some politicians who were using him to further their interests.

Nothing so far had worked right for Raju. How would he be able to leave Raju and Sally in the state they were in? His mind wandered to the various ways he had tried to have Raju treated. He had been made a pawn by believing the so-called Baba Dhilu. It was all a racket which he fell prey to. He was baffled.

The night went by, but Mahesh felt very uneasy. He just could not sleep. Kiran was still sitting in the living room, watching TV. It was a warm night with a slight breeze from the north. Mahesh stood beside the window and gazed outside at the forest, which housed myriads of insects, poisonous snakes, animals, birds and many other living organisms. The thick jungle covering the undulating lands looked scary in contrast to the city lights in the far distance. There was a shroud of darkness over where the dense jungle lay. A shrill cry of a coyote far away sent hundreds of birds flying away from their dens. He could hear their fluttering and dimly see their silhouettes against the open sky. The countless number of stars gleamed and glittered. It looked as if nature had ground up diamonds and sprinkled them over the endless blue space. The milky specks twinkled and danced along the sky in various patterns, making for a spectacular sight. It was almost midnight, and, apart from the odd cries of foxes or coyotes far away, the night was abnormally silent.

He lay on the bed, thinking about the chain of events that had transpired in the last few months. *What will happen if my visa to stay is not extended? How will Kiran and Mahek manage if Raju and Sally do not improve?* These thoughts slowly led him into a slumber. He had been dozing for an hour or so when the frightening, shrill scream of a woman echoed outside. Instantly, he sat up in his bed. Holding his head, he wondered if he really heard someone screaming. *I think I must be dreaming,* he mused and again lay down in his bed.

This time there was no mistaking it. It was a scream for help—a bloodcurdling scream, like the sound of a child wailing in pain. Hastily, Mahesh leaped off his bed, grabbed a torch and retrieved a shrub-chopping knife from the garage. He saw a startled Kiran looking at him from her bedroom door, as if telling him not to go. She must have been awakened by the scream as well. There was no time to waste. He swiftly climbed down the stairs and was out the door before anyone could stop him. Before he went out, he shouted to Kiran, "Please lock the door."

Then he was outside in the darkness. It was still firmly warm out. The trees stood utterly still, like statues in a living museum where no leaf dared to fall. He did not light his torch, but stood still outside the gate. A big tree trunk obscured his view of the house. Suddenly, a gust of wind came whistling around the trees. The clattering leaves and groaning tree branches gave him a creepy feeling. He could see the narrow road that linked the main road to the house.

To his surprise, he saw a shape like a car on that road. The glistening stars shone on the vehicle. Mahesh eased out of the shrubs, crouching with his eyes fixed on the target. He was about to light the torch when he thought he heard faint voices in the distance.

They came from the opposite direction. He retraced his steps back to the big tree he was standing under.

He advanced stealthily toward the place he thought the voices came from. There were strange stories about this jungle that ranged from people hearing weird sounds to people seeing white scurrying human figures.

Those must be the manmade illusions, he thought. Suddenly he became motionless. He could hear the rustling of leaves. It stopped—then it started up again, much nearer. It sounded like footsteps. Someone was walking toward him. With his mind focused, he huddled near a huge oak tree. There was definitely someone making a careful approach toward him. He tried to peek around the tree but it was too dark to see anything. There was a pause. Mahesh felt a chill running up his spine. Now the footsteps were in close proximity. He gauged that the presence was almost where he was.

He quickly stepped aside and flashed his torch light. A human-like figure clad in white robes scurried behind some bushes. It was scary. Mahesh shuddered at the sight. He could only make out the long, shabby hair. Otherwise, the figure was fully covered in white robes. Was it a woman? He flashed his torch uneasily. Could this be the same scurrying figure that people had sighted in the jungle before?

There was only one way to find out, he thought. He swiftly went behind the bushes where the figure went. But, alas, there was no one there. He inspected the place with his torch and found the dead leaves trampled upon. That gave him the reassurance that there was definitely someone out there—he hadn't imagined it. He stood there for some time and again the sound of people talking reached his ears. With utmost caution, he moved toward the source of the sound. Wind whispered through the branches and rustled the leaves, and hostile screeches from animals made the night very scary. He could feel light raindrops, but it did not dampen his spirit.

Suddenly, there appeared to be a scuffle, as dried leaves crackled under the weight of something. It could be a wild animal. The light wind carried the sickly stink of the dead vegetation and dried tree trunks. The smell of cigarettes and liquor suddenly made him more cautious. He moved faster now but with caution, ignoring the briars that caught at his jeans and the damp vegetation that licked at his skin.

Now he could clearly hear thumping and thudding sounds. The sound of leaves being trampled and a sudden human shriek scared the birds, which went fluttering out from their nests. It was unmistakably the sound of a woman. He could now see the glowing tip of a cigarette and crept toward it.

Mahesh sneaked a look between the thick shrubs. Just ten metres from where he was, there was a little clearing. He could make out two men trying to drag someone. Mahesh lurched forward and dived straight into them. He held one by the neck and pushed him hard on the ground.

Before he could rise fully, a fist landed on his right temple. But it was a light punch and did not do any damage. Immediately, Mahesh swung his right foot at the groin of that person. He doubled over in pain. The person on the ground was on his feet by this time. He advanced, cursing and spewing profanities. His left fist shot out like a rocket. Had it landed, Mahesh would have been done by now.

But Mahesh was waiting for such a move. He ducked and aimed a right blow that crushed the person's nose. That person staggered backwards. Before Mahesh could make any other moves, the second person rose and kicked hard at Mahesh's back. He reeled and fell to the damp ground. Both of them now advanced toward him. He knew he was no match for these two big guys. He groped for his knife but he must have dropped it during the scuffle. In a desperate attempt, he lunged at their feet. They went off balance and came crashing down. A mourning sound caught his ears. He flashed his torchlight. To his amazement there lay Sally—his own daughter-in-law. Her clothes were torn and smeared with mud. A scarf was tightly wrapped around her mouth. He could not see any more. A metal object hit him so hard that he lay flat, unconscious.

But he was not out of it for long. When his consciousness returned, he just lay there on the damp ground trying to place where he was. Without moving, he tried to rotate his eyes but could not. A man's voice then cut off his thoughts.

"Don't go wild, my sweetheart. Tonight, no one can stop me from getting you."

There was a scuffle again.

"Go away, you swine. You touch me and you are done!" cried Sally in a muffled voice.

"No, no, my sweetheart. Don't break my heart today. I won't hurt you, I promise." As he said this, Sally apparently kicked him hard since he groaned and cursed. Mahesh heard him cry, "You bitch!" Then, out of nowhere, the same white-clad figure appeared and gave him a blow to his head that sent him stumbling. He tried to control himself but could not. The force of the blow sent him slithering onto the wet red mud.

Mahesh wondered who that person in white was, as he was all alone again, against the duo. He shifted his gaze to Sally, who was being wrapped around by the same person. The condition she was in infuriated Mahesh. He went crazy with rage and, with clenched fists; he dived onto the second man who was now trying to lift his partner.

The man saw him coming and quickly moved aside. Mahesh landed flat-faced on the muddy ground. But he was very fast. In a swift movement, he put his leg against a big stone and hurled himself up onto his two feet. At the same time, a shot was fired. He felt a piercing pain as if his shoulders were on fire. The man opposite him raised his hand again with a gun pointed at him.

Mahesh thought this was the end. But the figure in the white robe hit the man with a stick. Mahesh could see a spurt of flame and the impact of that bullet sent him scrambling. Before losing consciousness, he heard police sirens and lot of flashing lights could be seen. He knew the cops were there now. He felt cold comforting hands and tried to open his eyes. The white-clad figure held him in its arms. In that last fleeing moment, he saw who that person was—it was Kiran.

***

It was almost three days later when Mahesh opened his eyes. The pungent smell of medicine and the pelting of raindrops on the windowpane awakened him. With slitted eyes he saw a ceiling fan rotating above him. Beside him there rested what looked like a wheelchair. Two armchairs were placed in a corner and a small table held several towels. "Where am I?" he murmured. He tried to lift himself up but a searing pain made him lie back down on the bed. When he looked to the other side, he saw several flower bouquets neatly arranged on a table. His eyes roamed around the room, but when he saw hospital equipment like oxygen bags, he knew this was a hospital. A slight groan from the adjoining room allayed his doubts. He tried to get up, but could not. He found his hands bandaged and his shoulder tightly wrapped with bandages. After several tries to get up failed, he finally lay still and closed his eyes.

He fell asleep again and slipped into dreamland. He saw Curly, who often used to play pranks on him. Mahesh was bathing in a small stream that meandered through his farm. All of a sudden, Sally appeared. She was smiling at him from the banks. He came out of the water to put on his clothes so that he could meet the love of his life. But the clothes were gone. Sally, who was standing on the banks a short while ago was now standing far away near the hills. She was waving at him with his shorts and

T-shirt. Mahesh quickly plucked some banana leaves from a banana plant that lined the stream and started running. The closer he got to Sally, the farther she appeared.

It started raining. Mahesh kept running with one hand holding the leaves that partially covered his lower body. He kept on running but could get no closer to Sally. She was jumping wildly and waving his clothes, as if teasing him. He finally got exhausted and started panting. He sat down on a rock. Sally was not visible now. The raindrops hit his face. Suddenly the cool rain turned warm. He started wondering: *How can cool raindrops turn warm all of a sudden?* The warm drops on his face kept on coming until he could bear no more. He tried to stand up but could not, so he forced himself to wake up.

With half-closed eyes, he could vaguely see a face staring at him. Another drop on his face awakened him fully. It was Kiran who was soothing his head and crying. Her tears rolled down her cheeks and landed on his face. With her was Mahek, who was staring at him with tears flooding her eyes. Mahesh tried to sit up but the sheer pain would not let him move. He forced a dry smile and groaned.

"Kiran and Mahek, are you okay?" Kiran quickly wiped her tears and sat beside his bed. Mahek edged nearer and put her hand on his forehead.

"Grandpa, you will be running soon. Believe me, Grandpa. I just talked to the doctor in charge. He said you are lucky. The injuries did not go deep and there are no broken bones. So nothing to worry about."

Mahesh knew she was comforting him. She reminded him of Curly—so caring and passionate. Well,

Mahek was her granddaughter. *Look at Kiran,* he thought. She was a stranger to him. But the way she cared and treated everyone with affection was beyond words. There was some kind of bond between them—an attachment so strong that it felt as if she was a reincarnation of Curly.

Kiran, meanwhile, collected all the "Get well soon" cards and read one by one to Mahesh. The first one was from Meena and Som. Then she read the cards from Raju, Sally, Kiran, and Mahek, and several from his friends in the temple. Mahesh was overwhelmed and emotional. He had so many good people who were with him during the bad times. With the help of Kiran and Mahek, he sat upright against some pillows. He cuddled Mahek for a while but because of his pain could not show his usual affection. Kiran fed him with some soup she prepared. Then Mahesh became silent, as he vividly recalled what had transpired in the jungle.

"How is Sally?" he inquired. Kiran smiled and recited the full chain of events that had ensued. She told Mahesh how she sneaked after him, not wanting him to know who she was, hence the white robes she wore over her head. When the fight broke out, she was the one to call the police.

"You took one bullet that just missed your chest and passed through your shoulders. The second one just greased you," she said.

"Yeah, because of you, Kiran. Had you not been there the first bullet would have done its harm. I can never repay you for what you did, Kiran," replied Mahesh.

He looked at her with deep gratitude. She blushed a little and looked away.

"By the way, did you ask Sally? How did she come to be in the clutches of those goons?"

Kiran looked up at him, expressionless. She helped Mahesh sip some water, after which she said, "Yes I did. They were not goons. They were her everyday friends with whom she went out to the clubs. They came to pick Sally up, but on the way they changed their minds when they saw Sally fully doped up. So they parked the vehicle on the road and grabbed her outside. Sally somehow managed to free herself and ran. But she could not run toward the house because they blocked her way. So she went straight for the bushes."

"Oh my God," exclaimed Mahesh. "I will not let them get away with this." Mahesh was seething with anger and his eyes turned red. "What happened to Sally? Is she badly hurt?"

"No, she is doing fine. They could not rape her. She just sustained some minor injuries," explained Kiran.

Mahesh was silent for a while. He was about to ask something else, when the sound of hurried footsteps outside the door distracted him. Sally was running with Raju behind her. Without any words, she just put her head on Mahesh's legs and started weeping. Mahesh looked at her helplessly. Before he could say anything, the doctor in charge entered and asked all visitors to leave as they were taking Mahesh for some scans and other tests.

***

Bhakti Place, where the temple was situated, was buzzing with activity. Men and women, both, were eager not to miss the general election the temple held every two years. This was an event for which people took leave from work in order to make their voice heard as they voted for the best possible candidate to lead the temple affairs. The hall inside was full to capacity. Not a single chair was vacant. There was an air of expectation and curiosity. Those present had no idea who the potential candidates for president would be. The current president, Atma Maharaj, was a very influential and popular figure in the area. People normally went with whatever he said—no questions asked. However, there were some who had reservations about Atma. They had reasons to believe that he was a corrupt and ruthless person, unfit to lead the temple affairs. Temple officials were seen scurrying up and down the stage that had been set up for the elections. Groups of people were chattering amongst themselves. Most of them believed that no one would have the guts to run against the current president. For them, he was the only one who could lead them.

A hush fell when the chairperson called the house to order. After a few preliminaries, all officials were asked to take their seats on the stage. Loud applause and cheers ensued when the current president, Atma, took his seat. That itself showed his popularity and grip on the people. People were surprised to see Granny in her wheelchair brought in by a security guard. She was ushered onto the stage beside the officials. People looked at her curiously, wondering why she was there. They did not know that she was one of the trustees of the temple and that Atma was her younger brother. The mayor of the city, Mr. Charles Chambers, was also seated onstage as the chief guest and scrutineer.

The election would be held under the supervision of two government officials seated in the aisle. After elections for the committee, the people were asked to call out the names of people they wished to be their incoming president. Several hands shot up. Atma Maharaj's name was moved to be the next-term president. The chairman of the elections asked for any other names. A hush fell. It was apparent that no one dared to move any other name for the presidency. Old Granny looked at the people, grinning. Atma stuck his chest out in pride. Those who did not like Atma could not speak up for fear of victimization.

"I wish to name another candidate, Mr. Chairperson." A croaky voice shattered the atmosphere. All eyes went to the speaker. It was an aged lady sitting in front. Her eyes were defiant and she appeared to be panting.

"I move the name of Mahesh Prasad as our new president." It was quickly seconded by a young man seated beside her. People were shocked as most of them did not expect any person to go against the ruthless Atma. People started murmuring and there appeared to be anxiety amongst them. One other gentleman stood up and voiced concern that any incumbent for the position needed to have experience and high moral values. Another interjected in support of his concern and added that Mahesh did not have a good reputation.

The chairman looked quizzically at the speaker, who was leering. Atma, who had appeared shocked when another name was moved, now seemed to be enjoying the ruckus.

"You must have a basis for your arguments, gentlemen. Just saying that a person does not have moral values holds no water," the chairman responded and looked inquiringly at the person who had opposed Mahesh's nomination. He now smiled sheepishly and looked at Atma, as if asking him to justify his arguments. Atma had the look of a tiger before it pounces on its prey. He chuckled and looked pleased.

One of his cronies again stood up. "Mr. Chairperson, how can the house elect a person who is not here? We need to have his acceptance first."

A number of people interjected. "Yeah, yeah. He is not here so he cannot participate in this election."

"Well, if that is the case, then the house cannot take his nomination," ruled the chairman.

"I am here, Mr. Chairperson," a voice cut in. It was Mahesh himself, limping his way toward the stage. He was using a pair of crutches and his hands were still bandaged. Some cheers and applause welcomed him but stopped as people saw Atma scowling at them. Old Granny peered at him in amusement—that amusement later changed to a puzzled look.

"Mr. Chairperson, I am a trustee of this temple and I do not hold the rights to take part in the election. Still, as an elder and a veteran of this temple, I do not think that Mahesh befits the position of the president."

Mahesh shot a shocked look at the old lady. He could not comprehend the reason for Granny's objection. Even the audience was shocked as Mahesh was now related to her.

"There must be a reason for your objection, ma'am. Why do you think the gentleman does not deserve the president's post?" asked the chairperson.

"Sir, the head of a temple should be a person who commands a lot of respect—a person who comes from the upper caste. Only such people can deliver services based on morals and ethics. Mahesh, here, is a person from a lower-caste family, so he should not be allowed to lead the temple affairs."

There was a surge of disapproval amongst the audience. People could be heard conversing with each other, denouncing the principles Granny upheld. However, they were too scared to voice their thoughts aloud.

Granny looked at them with evil eyes. "This applies to all of you over there." She pointed at the audience.

"If you are from an upper-caste family, you can contest this, but the temple is not for lower-caste people. You can all come and pray but leading is another matter."

This aroused a commotion amongst the public. People started shouting. One elderly person stood up and defiantly said that he would never support the ideals Granny was trying to spread.

"This is a place of God. No one is above the others here. Your deeds will tell you which family you are from. I completely object to what the old lady is saying. Mahesh is a person of experience and vision. He is educated and has a great vision for our temple. He just came from Fiji. In this short time we have seen how much he has done for the temple. I support Mahesh to be our next president." Most of the people stood up.

When Atma saw several of them talking against Granny, he quickly stood up too.

"Please be calm. Do not mind what Granny is saying. She is old and still has those old ideas." He chuckled.

Out of the corner of his eye, he saw the reaction of the people. Most of them nodded at what he said. Inwardly, he cursed them. They were all like sheep, he thought to himself. The voice of the chairperson rang out.

"Well, if there are no more names or objections, can we please go ahead with the election of the president?"

At that instant, a group of shabbily dressed people entered the premises. They placed themselves in every corner. Mahesh knew they meant trouble. They must be goons hired by Atma, who knew that he would lose the election if the contest proceeded.

Everybody took their seats again and waited anxiously.

"I have objections, Mr. Chairman." All eyes now shifted to the speaker who was none other than Atma himself.

He stood up with his chest out. "Mahesh, here, is a person with poor moral ethics. If you look at the police records, he was detained by the cops for harassing and sexually assaulting his own daughter-in-law."

A hush ensued in the hall. People gasped in surprise and disbelief.

"That is not true!" cried out Mahesh.

"It is true, Mr. Chairman. If need be, it can be vetted by his own daughter-in-law who called the cops to her own house," responded Atma.

"A person who does not have respect for his own daughters should never be a leader of any religious organization. I suggest that people like Mahesh should be ostracized from our community."

Atma was feeling overconfident now and was grinning. The venom on his face could easily be discerned, even from a distance.

Mahesh knew he was doomed. He did not expect Atma to stoop that low and make false allegations. Had it been someone else, it might have been palatable. But to watch a person whom people had faith in and who was regarded as a religious leader descend to that level—it was unbelievable.

Mahesh saw people eyeing him suspiciously. Atma had planted a seed of doubt which could later explode into hatred and distrust. The atmosphere was tense—very tense. Kiran and Mahek stood in one corner not knowing what to do.

Atma continued. "Mr. Chairman, this man came from Fiji a short while ago. Did anyone care to look at his past records? He may have committed similar offences there."

"Yeah, yeah," some of his cronies stood up to support Atma.

Mahesh was about to say something when Atma again lashed out at him. He was almost shouting now.

"He is a con man who has captivated some people with his sweet talk—a person who is a blemish on our society. He wants to be a leader here."

Atma pointed at Mahesh. "Mr. Chairman, he is a sexual maniac."

"LIAR!" A sharp female voice cut through the tense atmosphere.

People turned their heads to look at the speaker. They could not make out who it was. Once again the voice boomed, "Liar! The biggest liar and fraudster one will find on this earth!"

Atma's eyes nearly popped out of their sockets when he saw a young woman pushing her way through the crowd. Mahesh also shifted his gaze to the woman but could not recognize her. She was escorted by two males.

Like an athlete, she crossed the floor and took a stand on the stage much to the dismay of Atma and his cronies. The woman, wearing a red expensive *sari* and adorned with silver and gold jewellery attracted all eyes. They were glued to her beauty. She had a red round dot on her forehead, in the style of a traditional Indian woman. Mahesh took a better look and was shocked and surprised to realize it was his own daughter-in-law, Sally.

With the permission of the chairman, Sally waved to the people and introduced herself.

"To all our good people out there, what transpired in this meeting today should never be repeated." She quickly grabbed Mahesh and pulled him up near her.

"This is my father-in-law—but he is no longer an 'in-law' to me, he is my real father.

"He is a great person whom people should worship. A person who has taught us how important our culture and traditions are—a real father who can proudly be called a hero. Today, this lousy president who always glares at women had the gall to malign my dad."

Atma's face changed colour and he looked smaller. He glared at Sally with contempt and a cloud of despair engulfed him.

Sally continued. "Whatever he said here today is a lie. There was never a time when Dad made advances on me. No matter how rude I have been, he has always treated me like his own daughter. To say that he assaulted me sexually is a gross lie and has been uttered by this ruthless president just to sway your support. I am surprised that good people like you have been placing your faith in this scoundrel, whose own son-in-law tried to rape me."

The crowd grumbled and some people stood up. They were getting unruly and hostile.

"Order! Order, please," rasped the chairman. The people momentarily became quiet but they soon stood up again and crowded near the stage. There was a commotion. Some goons were seen pushing and pulling people. Fights broke out. People left their seats and dashed for the door. The meeting appeared to be in chaos. A pandemonium reigned with people seen running.

The chairman quickly ruled that the election had been postponed and would be conducted in the following week. Atma looked very happy. Maybe this was what he wanted—hence, the presence of the goons, thought Mahesh. Mahesh stood there speechless, looking at the frenzied people. Those goons intentionally created the furor. They even assaulted the man who spoke in favour of Mahesh. The security officers swiftly apprehended them, but, by then, the commotion had escalated into a rumpus. People pushed each other and ran outside for safety. Raju with Mahek and Kiran took Mahesh out back to the hospital. He was released a few hours earlier, following his incessant requests.

That night while lying in bed, Mahesh mulled over the day's events. He used to have respect for Atma, but today he craved to slap him. Being a religious leader, how could one become so crazy about power? It was apparent that Atma would go to any lengths to retain his grip on the temple. If all religious chiefs became power-hungry like him, what would become of the religion they prophesized? *Is this why so many religious groups are falling apart?* he wondered.

CHAPTER FIVE

A week later, another meeting for the presidential election was called. Only paid members were allowed entry and more security officers were called to maintain peace and stability at the meeting. Mahesh was once again released from the hospital for the meeting only. Atma and his cronies gathered in one corner, talking frantically as if debating some issues. Only the chairperson and the election scrutineers were allowed on the stage with Granny seated in a corner, in her wheelchair.

All eyes were upon Mahesh when he limped into the hall. Upon seeing him, Atma rubbed his hands and sniggered. He looked very pleased with himself. Mahesh knew there must be something cooking in his mind. His eyes met those of Granny. She was staring at Mahesh. Sometimes he wondered why he had got himself involved in this mess. He could have just stayed away and lived a peaceful life. But he knew himself too well—he was different. He could not see or endure any injustice inflicted on him or other people.

Today, the gullible people of the temple were under the claws of Atma, who they thought was the best person to lead them. But little did they know that behind the curtain of religion, Atma was exploiting people and abusing his power. This was evidenced by his "two-eyed treatment" of people. There were so many complaints against him but people did not have the courage to speak out, the main reason being fear of victimization. Mahesh thought that if every person sat quietly overlooking the fact that evil was prevailing over goodness, then very soon only goons and villains would rule the world.

His brooding was cut short when the chairman called the house to order.

"Ladies and gentlemen, our last meeting had to be abandoned due to circumstances beyond our control. Today, we need to complete the process in a manner that is enshrined in the constitution of the temple." The chairman looked up. All eyes were upon him now. Atma looked very pleased, as if he had already won the election. Granny still had that defiant look of anger seething in her eyes. Mahesh shifted his gaze to the audience. Many familiar faces smiled back at him. Only Raju could be seen in the gallery. There were no signs of Sally, Kiran or Mahek.

"So, can we have the names for the president's post, please?" Once again, he looked up. There were a couple of hands showing. Atma Maharaj was the first contender, followed by Mahesh.

"Are there any objections?" asked the chairman.

Atma rose from his chair. "Sir, we have some information on Mahesh that will astound the house."

A sudden onset of frustration could be seen on the faces of the people. They wondered what kind of information Atma had now. Whatever he did have, he appeared to have revealed it in the last session.

With a sneering look, Atma continued. "Sir, this person whom people want to be the president ran away with a pundit's daughter back in Fiji. He is not wanted there. Now he is trying to do the same thing here. I told the house how he sexually assaulted his daughter-in-law in her house and was kept in a cell. This is enough to prove that Mahesh has violated many ethical standards and is unfit to lead the temple."

Mahesh did not lose his patience, opting to remain calm. The only thing he said was, "Mr. Chairman, if Atma can prove the accusations he has made, I will willingly withdraw my nomination."

"You don't have to, Dad." Sally came forward and stood near the stage. "Sir, with your permission, let me clarify for once and for all. The allegation he has made is totally false. I will provide you with the necessary documents that I acquired from the police. Given some time, I can also furnish written proof from the police in Fiji that Mahesh legally married Karishma in a temple." She sat down, looking inquiringly at Atma. He looked dismissive but managed to regain his composure when the chairman asked him whether the Sally's explanation was enough for him. He shook his head and stood up, looking enthusiastically at Mahesh. Facing the audience, he looked as if he had something very important to say.

"Sir, to be a post holder in the temple one has to be a bonafide resident of the country. Mahesh is not a citizen of this country and is here on a temporary visa. So, he cannot contest the election," said Atma triumphantly. He knew that the victory now was his, as there were no other contenders for the presidency.

This information came as a shock to Mahesh and the people. Those supporting Mahesh gasped and could not believe what Atma had just said. They looked helplessly at Mahesh, who they thought would deny this allegation. But he himself was astounded at this revelation. He felt his lips dry up and knew the end was imminent. He was suddenly rattled by a familiar voice.

"Mr. Chairman, I have a question. If a person here is on a temporary visa and he marries a woman who is a citizen, doesn't this give that person the right to vote or contest in religious and social entities?" It was Kiran who posed this question. This was the first time Mahesh saw Kiran so composed and serious.

"Yes, for the betterment of institutions that may be allowed."

Atma interrupted with a sneer. "Sir, I think this woman is wasting her time here. What has marriage got to do with this man whose wife died so many years back?"

"You are wrong, Atma," remarked Sally. "It does have an impact."

"Hahaha!" Atma burst out laughing. His laughter was mocking. But it did not have any effect on Sally. Pointing at Mahesh, Atma continued. "Now, please don't tell me that Mahesh has a wife." He once again erupted in laughter, the sound echoing down the hall as he bent over, slapping his knee repeatedly.

"Yes, he does," retorted Sally. Her response completely spellbound Mahesh. Why was Sally lying? What kind of drama was being enacted now?

Even the public in the hall were aghast. How could Mahesh have a wife? They had never seen Mahesh with his wife. Where was his wife? A puzzled group of people who supported Mahesh started mumbling.

Atma jeered at Sally.

"Mr. Chairman, this woman here is lying. As I said before, his wife perished In Fiji. He came here alone. I know his family very well because his daughter is married to my sister's son, Som." Granny, seated in the corner, nodded vehemently and chuckled.

"If he has a wife, where is she?" Atma questioned in a high-pitched voice.

"I am his wife," a female voice boomed. It was Kiran, who once again made herself conspicuous in the hall.

Mahesh felt his legs giving way. He almost tumbled to the floor with shock. His mouth gaped open and his heart appeared to have stopped beating. *What is Kiran up to?* he wondered.

Kiran defiantly looked at the people and her gaze rested on Atma. He could not meet her eyes.

"Mr. Chairman, he is my husband," said Kiran, pointing at Mahesh. "Does the house still need proof?"

"No need, ma'am. Your words are enough."

Mahesh looked at the audience and his eyes stopped on Mahek, who was signalling him to remain quiet.

The chairman shook his head. He then asked people to obtain their ballots and vote for either of the two contestants. It took almost two hours for the results to be finalized.

When the meeting reconvened, people anxiously waited for the results. A pin-drop silence ensued in the house. The fate of the temple depended a lot on who became the next president. All eyes were on the chairman now as he opened the file.

"Ladies and gentlemen, thank you for being with us today. We have at last conducted the eagerly awaited election successfully. The results are as follows: Mahesh Prasad received ninety votes whilst Atma received ninety-two votes. I therefore declare . . ." He could not complete his statement. The house erupted in cheers and applause. Several people from the audience jumped on the stage and lifted Atma in jubilation. He was now clearly seen leering at those who had supported Mahesh. The news media were swiftly snapping pictures. Mahesh stared in disbelief as a sudden chill swept through his spine.

The results came as a surprise because most people, including Atma, had thought that Mahesh would win. Mahesh had high hopes of sitting at the helm of the temple and improving upon its activities. He had certain plans that he wanted to implement—plans that would foster harmony and better relationships between them and the non-Indo Fijian groups in the country. But now, all his hopes were in vain. He looked at the people and thought some of them were two-faced. If it were not the case, he would have won by a landslide. But that was how people were, he consoled himself.

He felt disheartened. The volley of yells and cheers kept ricocheting through Bhakti Place. Kiran was equally stunned. She saw Atma gloating at her. Her hatred for him flared into anger. For her, that man was a vulture. She could vividly remember how he gained her confidence and coaxed her to work at his house. His looks always troubled her.

His greedy, lustful eyes had always made her uncomfortable but since he was the head of a temple, no one would ever anticipate that he had any evil desires. She therefore respected and trusted him.

One day he came home early, about an hour before his wife normally arrived. Sally was in the kitchen doing the dishes when she heard a sudden cry.

"Argh! Argh! Kiran . . . Kiran!"

She quickly ran toward his bedroom. He was on his bed writhing in pain. As soon as he saw her, he pleaded,

"Please, Kiran. Just take out this sharp needle that is stuck in my back—I can't reach it."

She ran to his aid. As soon as she bent to examine him, two strong hands clasped her back. The hold was so tight that she felt herself lifted and slammed down on the bed on top of Atma. She tried to struggle and free herself but could not. Two hands probed inside the light dress she had on. She could feel his fingers going for her breast and his lips closing down on her when the door of the house opened. Atma quickly released her. It was his wife who had come home a bit early. Kiran ran away to the kitchen. She did not set foot on those premises again. Until today, only Sally knew of this incident. Kiran did not tell any other person what transpired, for fear of being maligned in public.

Amidst the yelling and whooping, the atmosphere suddenly went chill again. Sally, who had quietly sneaked out, now walked in with a pistol in her hand. She raised her hands and pointed her pistol at Atma. His eyes went wide in astonishment.

People gaped at her. "Is she going to shoot someone?" one bystander mumbled. Another ducked under the table. Some started panicking, but Sally shouted for everyone to remain calm.

She swiftly showed her credentials to the chairman, who gasped in astonishment. Soon after, a group of cops led by none other than Andrew followed her. Atma saw Andrew and wondered what he was doing with the officers. He had no idea that Andrew was also an undercover police officer. The cops accosted Atma and, before he could speak, he was handcuffed. He was totally shaken and struggled to say something, but could not utter a word.

Sally faced the audience and said, "Folks, I am Sally Prasad, an undercover detective and this here is Andrew Ryan, an undercover police officer. For the past two years, we have been working hand-in-hand to investigate the fraudulent practices being held behind the curtain of this temple. Some ninety thousand dollars' worth of deities made of pure gold was unearthed from the bushes. All the golden idols that were brought here for worship were cleverly replaced by Atma and his followers. In lieu of those, fake ones were put—the ones that you see now."

People could not believe what she was saying. They just stared at her with stupidity showing on their faces. Their eyes rolled up in incredulity.

"Atma," she continued, "is also charged with obtaining money under false pretences. He is the one who exploited people by telling them that he was Baba Dhilu, a witch doctor with divine powers."

Mahesh was again shocked. Now he understood why the voice of this fake Baba sounded familiar. So this was him, he mused. Sally continued.

"Andrew became his trusted friend and recorded his everyday activities. He baited the victims and asked them about their problems before bringing them to this fake 'Baba.' He briefed Atma before bringing the people to him for his services. This is the reason 'Baba' could tell people what their problems were without asking them any questions. Hence, people were impressed by this so-called divinity and saw 'Baba' as a person with great powers. Atma is such a low-down person that he even made passes at my daughter, who is like his own child."

The crowd started mumbling. Some angry faces could be seen scoffing at Atma.

"Above all," she continued, "he is also being charged for attempted rape. He assaulted a woman and tried to rape her. I should not be saying all this here, but because some of you see him as your 'messiah,' I thought it wise that you know the whole truth."

Angry voices lashed out from the hall. "Beat him—he is an animal!" People tried to surge forward in a fit of anger. The cops, however, calmed the people down and advised them to let the courts do their justice. Mahesh just stared at Sally, his daughter-in-law. He was proud of her for being so daring and courageous.

As Atma was being taken out, Granny obstructed their path. She was his eldest sister—more like a mum to him. Upon seeing her, Atma became emotional and tried to touch her feet for forgiveness, when a sharp slap brought him to his knees.

"You snake!" she lashed out furiously. "All this time I was mocking and belittling people from the lower caste, advising others that only people from upper-caste families have high moral values."

"I know, I know, sis. I have committed a mistake for which I am prepared to repent. But you being my sister and mother, please pardon my mistakes."

He looked pleadingly at Granny. She did not look at him but appeared to stare into space. It was a look of emptiness—the type of look one had when staring at nothing in particular.

"Today you have proved to the world that no matter which kind of family one comes from, it is their deeds and conduct that determine their character. You have let me down badly and have totally crushed the ideals I believed in."

She was crying. Tears rolled down her cheeks in a continuous flow. It was apparent that she was deeply hurt. Her hair was loose and looked shabby. Wiping the tears from her cheeks, she said, "You have shamed not only yourself, but your full upper-caste clan here and in Fiji. For what you have done, there is no repentance, Atma.

"I can forgive you, but not the Almighty up there." She looked at him one last time and said, "Go, rot in hell," and quickly ushered her wheelchair away from them.

Mahesh could not recover from the shock of the past events and just blinked in disbelief at all the surprises he'd just been exposed to. He felt dizzy and held on to the post he was leaning against. Slowly, he sank on the floor, slipping into unconsciousness.

***

It was Mahek who was sobbing. Her hiccups and random coughing stirred Mahesh. He quickly sat up in the hospital bed and stroked her.

"What happened my dear? Mahesh tried to soothe her. She immediately came into his arms and her sobs turned into a relentless cry. Mahesh thought she was crying because of him being hospitalized. After some time when she did not stop crying, he shook her. “C’mon, Mahek, you are a big girl now.” He lifted her head and wiped tears from her cheeks. Her eyes looked swollen. With reddish eyes she looked up at him.

Mahesh saw deep lines on her face. Instantly, he knew she had a problem. “Tell me what the problem is, Mahek.”

She didn’t speak for some time and looked weary.

“Grandpa, I need your advice. I have a boy in my life with whom I wish to settle after my graduation, but Mum and Dad do not approve of my choice.”

Mahesh frowned and then smiled passionately.

“But why wouldn’t they approve? You chose the boy—he must be a good person. Your choice is always the best.”

“It is not the boy. It is his caste and religion they are against, Grandpa.”

Mahesh was indeed jolted. He just hoped that Mahek had made a wise choice. As for religion and caste, that should not be a concern, he mumbled inwardly. One thing he knew was that it would be an uphill battle for him to go against all his family members. In any event, he would do it.

“Who is this boy, Mahek?”

“Grandpa, you have met him several times. He is the same person who is helping Dad, Dr. Sam Naivalu.”

Mahesh looked surprised but was prepared for anything.

"He proposed to me and I have very strong feelings for him." Mahek looked worried and looked pleadingly at Mahesh. "Grandpa, there is one more thing I wish to say."

Mahesh lifted his eyebrows and looked at her.

"If Mum and Dad do not agree to this relationship, then we will buy a house and live like partners, similar to the way boyfriends and girlfriends live. Once we are ready, we will do the religious marriage."

"No!" Mahesh snapped. Mahek was taken aback by the hostility that showed on her Grandpa's face. This was the first time he had been so harsh with her. Tears rolled down her cheeks.

Mahesh controlled himself and regained his composure. He put a hand on hers.

"My dear, do not ever make this kind of mistake. It is completely wrong and unethical." Mahek just looked at him with an innocent face.

"But why, Grandpa? So many of my friends live like partners under one roof, sharing the same room. What is wrong with that?"

Mahesh again felt a surge of anger arising. He walked to the window and looked outside. After a pause, he looked back at that honest and naïve face. He knew very well that many couples in this country lived together for several years, after which they decided to wed in a grand ceremony. He walked back and sat beside Mahek.

"You are the best in every way, my child. Parents dream of having children like you. I never want to see you do anything that may tarnish the culture and beliefs we embrace. In our custom, a couple should not have physical contact or dalliances before the religious marriage ceremony."

Mahek listened to him in silence. Her expression was that of a schoolgirl listening to her teacher. Inwardly, she felt shattered. Her hopes of living with her lover vanished, but still she wanted to know Grandpa's final verdict. He was the only one who would be able to make her wishes come true.

Mahesh continued. "Living in a Western country does not necessarily mean that we can abandon our traditions. In marriages, there are vows that have to be taken around the fire. The purity of a person, especially the girl, is always looked upon very seriously. Living together and marrying afterwards is like putting the cart before the horse. I have a lot of faith in you, my sweetheart, and I know that you will never let me down."

Mahek listened to him in amazement. She had great respect for him and always sought his advice before embarking on any new ventures. But today her emotions overrode the facts of life. She was dry-lipped and fought hard to say something.

"Do not worry, Grandpa. I will never let you down. You have told me before that girls are the epitome of respect for a family. I am proud to have you in my life. My parents are against my choice for a life partner. I will abide by what they want." She hesitated for a moment. Mahesh could see tears cascading down her cheeks.

"If this is how it must be, Grandpa, then I have decided not to ever marry."

She ran out of the room, wiping her tears. Mahesh was stunned and sat speechless, watching her scurry down the hospital hallway. He felt sorry for her. But what else could he do?

So many young people nowadays looked at marriage as a showcase. If they wanted to live together before having a religious marriage, then it was better for them to have a courthouse wedding and live together like husband and wife. They should then forget about Hindu rituals and ceremonies and refrain from having a grand, showy wedding. It was good to have an open mind and liberal views, but to stoop so low as to show disrespect to this significant religious ritual was just unpalatable.

***

The cool wind blowing on his face made him feel relaxed and cheerful. It was two months later and he was returning home. Home, sweet home, where Sally, Mahek and Kiran were waiting patiently for his arrival. Al least that was what he thought.

Raju was taking him home today. He would miss the memorable times and laughs he had with the hospital nurses and patients. The injuries he sustained in the incident in the field had healed with few scars and minor pain lingering in his legs. He was now declared physically fit to engage in light duties. That feeling of going back home boosted his spirit and wiped away any pain that remained.

He looked at Raju in the driver's seat. It was a different Raju. He looked healthy, and, with his muscles protruding from his T-shirt, quite athletic. Clean-shaven with neatly styled hair, Mahesh now saw his Raju looking the way he always wanted to see him.

"So Raju, how is your treatment going? Does that doctor still look after you?"

Raju looked at his dad's face and threw him a smile. He now had a thin moustache that complemented his charming personality.

"I feel so good now, Dad. No more drugs or smokes. I just can't express my gratitude for what you've done, Dad."

Mahesh could sense a deep affection in his son's voice. He was so relieved to hear this. At last Raju had realized his mistakes and was now on the correct path. He wished that Sally could also change her lifestyle to give them the perfect Indian family.

Their big house stood conspicuously amongst the thick vegetation. It could be seen from miles away. The driveway that meandered through the jungle was nearly free of potholes now and surrounded by neatly arranged planted trees. The lawn itself had been beautifully landscaped, adding even more beauty to the newly painted house. The last rays of the afternoon sun appeared to be playing hide-and-seek on the window glass. Even the once-dilapidated wire fence had been repaired. Mahesh was spellbound by the changes that had been made to the house.

"Here we are, Dad. You go inside. I'll just park the care and come in later," said Raju. He dropped Mahesh at the front door and eased his car slowly toward the garage.

The first peculiar aroma that hit Mahesh's nose was the fragrance of the incense sticks. It appeared as if someone was praying. Maybe it was Mahek, he mused. The living room was semi-dark and there was no one in there. He thought he would receive a warm welcome from his close-knit family. After so many weeks, he was back and there was no one to receive him. He found his heart sagging and a surge of loneliness gripped him. He was about to take another step when his eyes were blinded as though a thousand flashlights had been turned on at the same time. It was, in fact, the brightly lit new chandeliers that now hung from the ceiling. Voices echoed in chorus.

"Welcome home! Welcome home! Oh, our dear one!"

Running footsteps could be heard from all sides. Mahek was the first one to hug him, followed by Meena, Som and Kiran, who blushed slightly at the sight of him. Even old Granny in her wheelchair greeted him by clapping. The clapping intensified when all joined hands and greeted Mahesh. He felt very happy but he was a bit restless. His gaze went around the room, apparently looking for something. Meena saw her dad looking a little uneasy and wondered whether he was expecting someone else. Why was he looking so fidgety?

But his uneasiness faded immediately when he saw what he wanted to see. Sally, once again dressed neatly in a *sari*, was holding a brass tray in which a piece of camphor was burning. She slowly made her way down the steps. Every person in the room was astounded to see Sally in this form. Holding a section of *sari* over her head and with a red round blot on her forehead, she presented herself in a manner that caused even her own husband to stare at her agape. With her kohl-black hair cascading over her shoulders, a different Sally was seen today. Her captivating and charming smile and elegant posture with her eyes cast downwards made Mahesh feel very proud.

Sally stood in front of him with a bowed head, then slowly looked upwards at Mahesh and started circulating the brass tray with its burning camphor around Mahesh. This was a typical Indian way of offering love, benevolence and respect to one's elders. All eyes were on Sally now. She put the tray down and put a wee bit of sandalwood paste on Mahesh's forehead, after which she knelt and put her head at his feet. He could not believe his eyes and stared at her, bewitched. She started sobbing with convulsive gasps. Mahesh felt uncomfortable and tried to move but she held his legs with her hands and cried her heart out. Her cries echoed through the living room and made the whole atmosphere sentimental. Tears could also be seen rolling down the cheeks of Kiran and Mahek. Meena quickly came forward and lifted Sally to her feet. Her face was red and blotchy. Mahesh patted Sally and soothed her.

"Calm down, my child. If you have a problem, let me know. We all are with you, my dear."

Sally looked up with reddish eyes and tried to speak. She appeared to have a lump in her throat and her voice cracked when finally she spoke. "Dad, I just want to apologize for the grave sin I have committed. I ridiculed you, swore at you and made your life so uncomfortable, and yet you risked your life to save me from those goons."

"That's okay, my dear. Any person would have done what I did. I never took your rude remarks seriously, since I know that there was no one to guide you after your mum's death. Even Raju did not pay enough attention to you." Mahesh smiled passionately at her. Sally just looked at Mahesh with wet eyes. Kiran came closer to the duo and wiped her own tears before speaking.

"It is true, Mahesh, that Sally was orphaned at a young age. When she came here the only friends that she had were the ones who regularly take her to the pub. They are the ones who led her down the wrong path. I did my best to help her but she became very high on herself and dismissive after becoming a police detective."

Kiran hugged Sally and with comforting words continued. "She is now a changed woman. A person who is disciplined, cultured, and one who commands immense respect—thanks to Mahesh."

Sally quickly turned around and gave a beaming smile. Raju came forward and embraced Sally. Even Granny eased her wheelchair next to Sally and congratulated her. She looked at Mahesh. Her eyes showed signs of remorse and respect. Very softly she spoke.

"Mahesh you have also opened my eyes. I was so wrong and always discriminated against lower-class people. I have seen what my brother has done."

Disappointment lingered on her face. In lieu of the fiery eyes that were always there before, a shade of sadness lurked in them.

"Please forgive me. I am an illiterate old woman and have been exercising what my elders taught me. But, together, your words of wisdom and the memories of past incidents have made me realize how wrong I was."

Her husky voice no longer held any arrogance or boldness. She was almost on the verge of crying. Mahesh quickly cut her short.

"No, Granny—you were just doing what you were told to do. Our ancestors, being illiterate, were often misguided by the people in authority. They embraced loyally what they were made to believe. So, please do not blame yourself."

Granny took her eyes off Mahesh and gazed at the others who were all looking at her with respect. She nodded in agreement with what Mahesh just said.

"Yes, you are correct Mahesh. But you don't know how many mistakes I've made. I just hope I did not mistreat anyone," she mumbled and steered her wheelchair away from Mahesh. To liven up the atmosphere, Mahesh cracked a joke about how they once went to a sugar cane field to poop and then ran when the farm was set on fire deliberately by a neighbour. He cracked several other jokes much to the pleasure of all present. Even Granny could be seen laughing. The sombre atmosphere that prevailed was now replaced by a cheerful ambience. Raju was seen humming in the kitchen with Sally and Kiran. Good news had come their way in the form of Mahesh's visa being extended. He was given another two years to stay.

Everyone appeared to be happy and content except Mahek, who just stood in the corner and pretended that she was happy. Mahesh was quick to discern the sadness on her face. He knew through experience that Mahek was just trying to hide her true feelings and that she was, in fact, deeply hurt.

At the dinner table, Mahesh learned how Atma and his cronies had been charged and jailed for the temple racket. They had stolen some ten thousand dollars in cash from the offerings people gave to the temple, not to forget the expensive golden idols that they had replaced with false ones. His son-in-law was also arrested, along with one other person, for attempted rape and assault with a deadly weapon. Sally was now the acting president of the temple and worked hand-in-hand with the head priest.

Mahesh now stared at Kiran, who quickly put her eyes down. She even stopped chewing the food she had in her mouth. Mahesh just smiled at her and asked, "There is one thing I cannot understand, Kiran. Why did you lie in the meeting and say that you were my wife?" She again blushed and fidgeted in her chair. Eyes downcast, she answered in a soft voice.

"There was no other way to shut those people up. It is said that one lie cannot be seen as a sin if it is made to establish righteousness in society."

She now looked up and saw Granny gaping at her. She quickly shifted her gaze to Sally.

"That was a big move by you, Aunty—we are all so proud of what you tried to do," said Sally. Mahesh also felt proud of Kiran.

Mahek, who used to be so bubbly and loquacious, just looked at them with no expression. She quietly excused herself and took her dishes to the sink. Without looking back she made her way to her bedroom.

Mahesh suddenly became serious and cleared his throat as he spoke.

"There has been something bothering me for a while, Raju and Sally." All eyes turned toward him now, as he looked very concerned.

"Mahek has chosen her life partner and you did not agree to her choice. Can I ask you why?"

Raju and Sally looked taken aback. They had no idea that Mahek had told Mahesh about her intentions.

"Dad, now that you know about it . . . Do you know the boy she has chosen?" replied Raju.

Sally quickly interrupted. "Dad, the boy she has chosen is from a different race. Even his religious beliefs are different. How can we allow our daughter to marry a person from a different racial background? The boy is a Fijian."

Mahesh glared at them with a frown on his face. On one hand, he was happy for his beloved granddaughter, while on the other, he had to answer to society. He eventually spoke.

"Honestly speaking, I don't see anything wrong with that. For me, race, caste and religion should not be a factor in determining a life partner."

"What are you saying, Mahesh?" growled Granny. "How can you give the hand of your grand-daughter to a Fijian boy? You have so much respect in the society. Don't you know that they will castrate you and the whole family for allowing this?"

She looked angry now and Mahesh could see her panting. With her eyes aflame, she stared at Mahesh. He calmed down Granny with his hands and got up.

"Well, if that is the way you all want it, I can't say much. But, please remember, if she is not married to that doctor, she will still live with him under one roof."

All eyes went wide in surprise. Granny wanted to say something but could not. Even Sally and Raju were at a loss for words.

"This trend is fairly common now in Western lands and our people are fast taking this on board—live together after which show to the world your pompous wedding."

"How can that happen? Are they crazy? How can they have a religious wedding after living together? It is strictly taboo in our culture." Granny again started panting.

Mahesh remained quiet and sensed that discussing this issue with Granny around would be futile, so before leaving the dinner table, the only thing he said was, "I do hope that common sense prevails. If all of you are against the marriage, that's your choice. But remember the consequences could be really bad."

He wished he could do something for Mahek. Now all his hopes had faded and he could envisage a future full of scorn and criticism directed at his family. *Well,*

I am not going to impose anything upon the family, he mumbled inwardly.

Later at night, Mahesh could be seen having a long discussion with Raju and Sally. What eventuated was anybody's guess.

CHAPTER SIX

The college auditorium was full to capacity with people from all walks of life.

Parents, friends and colleagues of the students graduating today, thronged the hall striving to get a better seat in front. Even friends of Mahesh's from the temple joined the hustle and bustle. There was an air of excitement—an air of expectancy. The college students were all very nervous. This was the first year that they had not been advised of their passing grades. All were asked to attend the graduation. They did not know who would graduate. Those who had failed might have to walk out of the auditorium. Mahek was very tense and edgy.

Mahesh, along with Kiran, Raju, Sally and Meena, were seated in the second row. All the college students were seated together away from the audience. Light music filled the room amidst chattering and laughter. The hall was dimly lit as the curtains were still drawn across the several windows it had. Even a newcomer to such an event would have felt the tension that brewed, especially in the faces of the students who otherwise would have been bubbling with energy and excitement.

Today they all looked gloomy and worried. Fears gripped them. What if they did not graduate? People would laugh at them—they would be taunted by their friends and families. Those who passed and acquired their credentials today would be on top of the world.

All of a sudden, the main door to the stage was flung open. The music stopped and a pin-drop silence followed. The dean of the college marched in, followed by three other senior staff. He nodded at the audience and took his seat.

A chubby person with grey hair pasted down neatly on his head and donning a pair of glasses, the dean looked to be a very disciplined and strict person.

After the initial preliminaries by the dean, the principal thanked all the students, teachers and parents for their support. He then picked up a green file which had the results.

"Ladies and gentlemen, fellow teachers and students. It is a remarkable achievement for this college—a historic one I would say." He could not fully complete what he was saying before the students jumped with joy. They could sense what was coming. Cheers and loud applause followed.

The principal scowled at the students and waved at them to sit down. "I have not finished yet. This is the first time that not a single student—cough, cough, cough." He paused to have some water. The electrified atmosphere again turned sombre. Worried looks could be seen on the faces of the students once more. The principal, meantime, was drinking some water and still coughing. The students now believed that not a single one of them had passed the final exam. Some of them were on the verge of tears. One or two were about to sneak out the exit when the principal's voice again boomed in the hall.

"My apologies, folks. As I was saying, this is the first time in history that not a single student has failed." He could not go any further. The cheers and applause rocked the room. Some of the parents even stood up and started jumping along with the students.

One by one, the students were called onto the stage and offered their credentials. Cameras flashed and families and friends scurried to get their photos. Mahek walked nervously on the stage to get her certificate. Mahesh stood and started clapping.

At that very moment, a loud bang sounded and the hall lights went out. It was followed by another bang—a gun shot. Mahesh felt a bullet race past his ear. It studded into the board behind the stage. At the same time he shouted, "Dive for cover! Dive for cover!" A series of shots rang out. The hall was full of cries now. People toppled each other and ran outside for safety.

Mahek attempted to run from the stage. The third shot would have taken Mahek point-blank had it not been for a man who flung himself on top of him and took Mahek down. Briskly, the man got to his feet and crouched in the darkness. It was then that Mahesh caught a fleeting glimpse of two men in masks, holding their guns and making their way toward where Mahek was lying. He knew now that their lives were in danger. He was not worried about himself. His only worry now was Mahek. Out of the corner of his eye, he saw the two men almost on the stage. Raju was on their heels. He pulled one down on the floor, tearing his collar. When he saw his partner going down, the first assailant pointed his gun at Mahek and was about to press the trigger, when a flying kick tore the gun from his hands. The gun went flying ten feet away. He was about to get up when an open-palmed slap to the man's face shattered his nose, causing it to bleed profusely. Mahesh could now recognize the man. It was the same stranger who had pushed Mahek to safety. He quickly lifted her up and ran outside. In the meantime, the cops arrived in numbers and accosted the two thugs who wanted to kill Mahesh and his family.

Mahek was not hurt but she was badly scared and was trembling. Upon reaching her, Mahesh found the stranger to be the same doctor who had treated Raju—Dr. Sam Naivalu.

After several months it was found that the assailant who led the attack was the son of Atma, Krit Maharaj—

the same young man who could not defeat Mahek in the last oratory contest. Like his father, he was also sent to jail.

***

It was Father's Day in the country—the day that celebrated all the fathers in the world. Raju and Sally hosted a party. Outside friends and families were also invited for dinner.

Kiran, Mahek and Sally were busy in the kitchen, preparing. Only Sally's voice could be heard and she appeared to be in good humour. Mahesh shot a glance at Kiran, who appeared very sad as her in-laws were taking her back home tomorrow. She did not want to go, but after much persuasion from Mahesh she agreed to leave and get herself established.

Kiran's parents had arranged a relationship with a distant family widower who was disabled and wanted to have a life partner. Kiran shuddered at the thought since that person was an aged man of seventy. From the time she had agreed to go, she had been crying.

Mahek was also mostly sad these days. Sombre and quiet, she was often seen with wet eyes. Mahesh could feel her pain and wished he could do something for Mahek, and even Kiran. But there were few things in life that one had to compromise on in order to excel. Mahesh suddenly received a phone call from Fiji. He talked to somebody for a while, and, as he put down the receiver, he became thoughtful. He quietly went to his room and stood beside the window facing the vast stretch of jungle. With squinted eyes, he just looked out at the open space. After a while, he appeared to be content and a little smile crossed his face. He summoned Raju and Sally to his room. They talked for about half an hour and no one could guess what they were talking about. Relatives and friends started pouring in for the evening get-together.

A big table was set up with all types of delicacies. Meena, Som and Granny joined them for the occasion. The house once again became cheerful and lively. Gifts were offered to the fathers who came. Sally brought an envelope on which was written "DAD—OUR SUPERHERO." Before handing the envelope to Mahesh, she gestured for everyone to be quiet.

"Thank you for coming and sharing this great day. Today, I, along with my husband, Raju, wish to pay tribute to a great man. I would say the greatest of all, our dad, Mahesh. When he first came here, I acted like a jerk and didn't give him the respect he deserved. In fact, I became too Westernized and forgot that I still am a married Indian woman. Today, my life and my and Raju's life, has completely changed due to the ideals and sacrifices our dad has made during his stay so far."

Looking at Mahesh, she continued with tears in her eyes. "Dad, once again, I am sorry for what I did in the past. Had it not been for you, our lives would be miserable. Thank you, Dad." She bowed down and touched Mahesh's feet. Raju followed likewise. Wiping her tears, she handed an envelope to Mahesh. There were two keys inside.

Sally smiled with affection and said, "Dad, one key is for the brand-new car we bought for you and the other key is for the room beside yours. It is a small temple we have created for all of us to pray."

Mahesh was dumbfounded. Not only was he surprised, but he was equally shocked. He just looked at Raju and Sally with heartfelt emotion and said,

"Thank you, my kids. You guys are awesome. To all my friends and relatives, thank you. Please bear in mind that in our custom, Father's Day is every day. It does not necessitate material gifts. The gift every father wishes to have is to see his children excelling in life and becoming respected people in society."

Big applause filled the room. He continued.

"Many people who come to Western countries completely eradicate their beliefs and cultures. They often overlook the richness these cultures cultivate. I commend Sally for opening a Hindi school in the temple. This will give our people an opportunity to learn our mother tongue, especially the kids born here. There are people who go to other countries and try to impose their own practices forcefully. This, in my opinion, is not justified. As Mahek said in her oratory competition, we should learn to be flexible. Respect others, their religion, their beliefs, and modify ours where necessary. With a give-and-take attitude, we can conquer the world."

There was another round of applause. Old Granny was so moved by his speech that she tried to stand up, but to no avail. However, she raised her hand and said "God bless you."

Mahesh saw Mahek sitting alone holding her head with both hands. She did not look to be interested in the event. Mahesh added, “I would like to make an announcement.” A hush fell over the room. All eyes were on him now.

“I have had a good discussion with Raju and Sally, and we all agree that Mahek, our daughter, will have to leave this house by next year.”

“What?” cried Mahek. She came running over to her grandfather. Holding his hand, she said, “But what did I do that you are asking me to leave this house?”

She could not control the flow of tears that started coursing over her cheeks.

“Why am I being treated this way?” She went to Raju and started pulling at him. “Please, Dad, tell me why are you doing this to me? Why? Why? Why?” she cried and slid onto the floor, weeping.

The guests in the room were moved by her reaction. What wrong did Mahek do? She was one of the best people in the family and yet they were kicking her out of the house? Mahesh slowly lifted Mahek and put his hands on her shoulders. He looked in her eyes and said, “Because we have chosen a boy for you to get married to next year.”

The news came as a shock to Mahek. Her heart seemed to stop. She was at a loss for words, as she had a man in her life—a person whom she had chosen to be her life partner. But now her parents were forcing her to marry a boy of their choice? She would not stand for this. But out of respect, she could not open her mouth to speak against her elders. How could she ever think of living without her lover, Doctor Sam?

Didn't these elders understand that a girl falls in love only once? She was in love and they knew it, yet she was being treated like child, she observed silently. Her face grew pale and in lieu of tears in her eyes, there was determination. *I will do as my parents want me to do,* she decided, and stood still, staring at the wall devoid of any expression. Mahesh again spoke. "We have decided to have Mahek engaged to none other than Dr. Sam Naivalu."

The roar of applause that followed was deafening. Mahek, her eyes wide open, flung herself at Mahesh. "Oh, Grandpa! I just love you."

She suddenly started sobbing as she could not handle the unexpected news and abundance of happiness which had overcome her. The faces of the other people in the room lit up. Mahek hugged Raju and Sally next, only managing to say, "Thank you." Mahesh's voice again boomed.

"Last of all, I wish to pay tribute to Kiran, who has been looking after this family more like a mother than a maid. She is one of the greatest women I have met in my life. No other outside person would have done as much as she did in this house." The people's gaze now shifted to Kiran, who started crying. Mahesh signalled Sally to bring Kiran forward. She stood near him with eyes downcast and tears falling down her cheeks. "Tomorrow she will be leaving to start a new journey in her life."

"No." A voice suddenly interrupted Mahesh. It was Raju. "She is not going anywhere. Dad, you asked us to agree to Mahek's engagement to Dr. Sam, but there was a condition you agreed to. You promised us that you would also agree to any future requests we would make."

Mahesh looked at Raju and smiled. "Yes, I remember Mahesh. I will definitely accede to your request."

Both Sally and Raju came beside Mahesh and said in one voice: "Please, Dad, marry Aunty Kiran and give her the life she deserves. Please, Dad."

"Oh my god!" said Granny. "What are you saying, Raju? Kiran is a widow and she cannot be with any other man in her life. You should not be going against our culture!"

"What culture are you talking about, Granny?" rebuffed Raju. "Are you talking about the culture that has been deriding women for ages? If her husband perished, was it her fault? Why are we ruining her future? She has every right to live like any other woman. The society that embraces this outrageous and brutal principle that widows cannot remarry or live a happy life has to take another look at their principles," said Raju.

"Exactly," Sally cut in. "We should learn from our friends in this modern country where women are treated justly. We cannot and should not uphold these archaic and unjust policies that degrade humane values. Men and women, both, are equal."

Granny just looked at them, not knowing what to say. She nodded and was about to respond when Sally again spoke. "Just think, Granny. If this was your own daughter, would you just sit back and watch her suffer?

Day and night, she labours and puts a smile on everyone's face. Doesn't she deserve a better life?"

Old Granny had tears in her old eyes. A surge of pain crossed her face. In a faint and husky voice she said, "Yes, I guess you are correct. I cannot forget my own daughter being ill-treated by society when her husband died. My eyes should have opened then."

Looking at Mahesh, she continued, "What are you waiting for? Accept her and give her a life, Mahesh."

Mahesh was confused. He felt embarrassed, too. Internally, he loved Kiran, but could not divulge that feeling. But now, as things stood, he thought he'd better make a firm stand. He looked glowingly at Kiran and said, "Kiran, you do not know how much I love you. Will you accept me as your husband?"

Kiran's blushing face spoke volumes. She kept looking down at the floor, and, with great difficulty, she looked up. Her eyes were full of gratitude for this man. In a very soft voice she said, "I also love you, Mahesh." She lowered her eyes again and her face went ever redder. No more could be heard as cheers erupted and people thronged them from all sides with well wishes.

Raju, Sally, Mahek and Meena quickly grabbed Kiran and dragged her near Mahesh. Mahesh took Kiran in his arms. Mahek put her arms around Mahesh and said, "Our super dad—the hero!"

Granny chuckled and shook her head from the corner. "God bless," she said before retreating to the guest room.

CPSIA information can be obtained
at www.ICGtesting.com
Printed in the USA
LVHW021950240219
608605LV00005B/10

9 780228 808084